THE FORTU

SHIPMENT 5

Mendoza's Secret Fortune by Marie Ferrarella
The Taming of Delaney Fortune by Michelle Major
My Fair Fortune by Nancy Robards Thompson
Fortune's June Bride by Allison Leigh
Plain Jane and the Playboy by Marie Ferrarella
Valentine's Fortune by Allison Leigh

SHIPMENT 6

Triple Trouble by Lois Faye Dyer
Fortune's Woman by RaeAnne Thayne
A Fortune Wedding by Kristin Hardy
Her Good Fortune by Marie Ferrarella
A Tycoon in Texas by Crystal Green
In a Texas Minute by Stella Bagwell

SHIPMENT 7

Cowboy at Midnight by Ann Major
A Baby Changes Everything by Marie Ferrarella
In the Arms of the Law by Peggy Moreland
Lone Star Rancher by Laurie Paige
The Good Doctor by Karen Rose Smith
The Debutante by Elizabeth Bevarly

SHIPMENT 8

Keeping Her Safe by Myrna Mackenzie
The Law of Attraction by Kristi Gold
Once a Rebel by Sheri WhiteFeather
Military Man by Marie Ferrarella
Fortune's Legacy by Maureen Child
The Reckoning by Christie Ridgway

THE **FORTUNES** OF **TEXAS**

FORTUNE'S PERFECT MATCH

❧

NEW YORK TIMES BESTSELLING AUTHOR

Allison Leigh

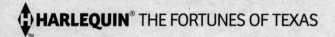

HARLEQUIN® THE FORTUNES OF TEXAS

Special thanks and acknowledgment are given to
Allison Leigh for her contribution to
the Fortunes of Texas: Whirlwind Romance continuity.

ISBN-13: 978-1-335-68044-0

Recycling programs
for this product may
not exist in your area.

Fortune's Perfect Match

Printed in U.S.A.

www.Harlequin.com

A frequent name on bestseller lists, **Allison Leigh**'s high point as a writer is hearing from readers that they laughed, cried or lost sleep while reading her books. She credits her family with great patience for the time she's parked at her computer, and for blessing her with the kind of love she wants her readers to share with the characters living in the pages of her books. Contact her at allisonleigh.com.

For my dad.
Still my favorite pilot.

Prologue

December

Jesus loves me, this I knoooow...

The verse of the lullaby that her mother used to sing circled around and around inside Emily Fortune's head.

Tears squeezed out from her tightly closed eyes. She'd closed them because of the dust and debris, but she knew if she opened them again, she would still be there in the dark.

Alone.

Jesus loves me, this I know...

She inhaled on a sob that ended in a choking cough.

She didn't know what had happened.

One minute they had all been walking through the airport. Her brothers up ahead while Emily tried to catch up to her mother—

She coughed through another choking sob. Where was her mother? Had the world collapsed on her, too? On all of them?

They'd been visiting Red Rock for Wendy's wedding.

More tears burned from the corners of Emily's eyes. Wendy. Her baby sister, who'd looked so beautiful and happy—finally, *finally,* happy and settled—as she'd exchanged vows with Marcos during their Christmas Eve wedding.

Had *all* of Red Rock collapsed? Were Marcos and Wendy and their baby that she was carrying lost, too?

Jesus loves me...

Emily covered her mouth, coughing again. Crying.

She wasn't a crier. She was a planner. A doer. Even her father admitted that about her. He'd often said that's what made her so valuable at her job at FortuneSouth.

But the only thought in her mind right then was that she was going to die.

Her feet were trapped. Numb. She could barely breathe. Couldn't even see her hand in front of her face. All she could hear were the screams inside her head that she couldn't even gather enough strength to let out.

What did it matter if she'd focused her whole life on becoming valuable to the family business?

She was going to die there, never knowing what had hit the *family,* never knowing if any of them were safe or not. She'd die, never feeling the joy that had been in her little sister's face as she said "I do" to the man she loved. She would never know how it felt to have the proof of that love growing inside her.

She'd never hold her daughter in her arms, rocking her to sleep the same way that Emily's mother had rocked *her.* She'd never calm a cranky, infant son with a lullaby. Never... never...never—

She coughed again as more dust suddenly collapsed onto her, sending off another round of shouting inside her head.

This was to be her only future, then. Ended beneath the rubble of a small, regional airport in southern Texas.

More dirt fell.

Even though there was no point, she curled her arms around her head. Light appeared beyond her eyelids. Beyond her arms. But there was no sense of peace coming over her. No sense of welcome.

Had she lived her life so wrongly that she wouldn't even have that? Just this choking, oppressive aloneness? No future?

She curled her arms tighter around her face. She tried to find the comforting lullaby again...but even the childhood song that had been circling over and over inside her head had deserted her.

And then she heard another shout. Not inside her head at all. Hands clutched her arms, pulling them away from her head. She stared, squinting against the light and the dust still clouding the air, seeing only the shape of a fireman's hat above her.

"What—" She broke off, coughing again.

He didn't seem to notice. "Get me some help here," he yelled, moving away from her.

She heard more voices. Realized that there were a lot of voices. Yelling. Some screams. She swiped her hands down her face. Squinted at her hands. All she could see was black. She tried to push herself up until she was sitting, but could only raise herself a few inches. There was a tangle of metal pressing against her entire right side.

"Hold on there." Another voice found her.

A different voice. Deeper. Gentler. Hands brushed against her, levering the metal off of her. A row of attached chairs from the airport's waiting area, she realized.

She tried to focus on the rescuer's face, but everything seemed blurry. Covered in gray. But his eyes...his eyes were blue. She latched desperately on to that blue gaze. "What happened?"

"There was a tornado." His hands circled her arms. Pulling, she realized.

"My feet." She couldn't utter more than that. Her throat had closed again; tears came harder.

He immediately stopped pulling. Shifted away from her vision. She wanted to call him back. She managed to push herself up a few inches and saw the man, gesturing at the fireman. Her strength gave out and she fell back. She could feel sobs clawing at her chest.

"Come on now." The voice was back. "You made it this far." He closed his hand around hers, squeezing gently. "You're pinned by something, but they're gonna get you out." The dust covering his face creased into lines around his mouth as he smiled. "You've got a future just waiting for you to live it."

Chapter 1

June

"I'm sorry, Dad. I'm not flying back to Atlanta tomorrow just to handle one meeting. It's completely unnecessary." Emily's hand tightened around her cell phone and she gave Wendy a rueful grimace. "I'll join in by conference call."

Even through the phone line, she could feel her father's irritation. John Michael Fortune had always expected his employees at Fortune-South Enterprises to give him more than a hundred percent of their attention, and his children who worked for him were no exception.

"There's no reason for you to still be in Red Rock," he stated. "It's June, for God's sake. Wendy had that baby months ago. I think even she might have learned how to heat a bottle and change a diaper by now."

Emily winced. She held the phone closer to her ear and hoped to heaven that Wendy—who was sitting in a lovely white glider near the nursery's window—couldn't hear. And even though tiny MaryAnne *had* been born in February, she'd still been early.

Emily focused on the baby's perfectly shaped head as Wendy slowly rocked and nursed.

That's what mattered, she thought to herself. "There's nothing on my plate that I can't handle long-distance," she said into the phone. And there wasn't. She was the director of advertising for their telecommunications company, and whether John Michael gave her many accolades or not, she knew she was doing her job well.

Business was booming, after all.

"I don't know what's gotten into you," her father muttered, still clearly dissatisfied. "Ever since that tornado, nobody's been the same. And you, with this baby nonsense—"

"People died in that tornado, Dad," Emily

cut him off, not wanting to hear the rest. *They'd* all been the lucky ones, but there were others who hadn't been so fortunate. Emily had ended up with only a sprained ankle. Her mother, thankfully, only a broken wrist. "It's sort of a life-changing experience, you know."

She heard his enormously frustrated sigh. "Fine," he snapped. "Conference into the meeting this time. But I'd better see your face on Friday at the first Connover meeting."

For a fleeting moment, Emily was tempted to ask what the unspoken "or else" was, but she fought the urge. Yes, she was bristling at the iron hand of her father's management, but that didn't mean she didn't still respect his position both as her father and as the head of FortuneSouth. "I've already got the charter flight scheduled to be there," she promised. "Say hello to Mother for me."

"Say hello yourself," he returned bluntly. "She's missing all of you a lot these days, since it seems half her family is deserting Atlanta for Red Rock."

Emily's grip tightened on the phone again. She talked to her mother regularly, and John Michael knew it. Like her father, her mother didn't entirely understand Emily's actions these days, but, typically, she'd been far less critical about it. "I love you, Dad."

"Friday," he returned.

She sighed and hit the end button on her phone. Even under the best of circumstances John Michael wasn't an affectionate soul. She looked over at Wendy. "Do you ever wonder what on earth attracted our parents to each other enough in the first place to get married *and* have six children together?"

Wendy smiled a little impishly. "Frankly, Em, I don't *want* to think too much about Mom and Dad getting busy making babies." She leaned down to kiss her daughter's perfectly pink forehead. "I prefer to think we were all immaculately conceived."

Emily smiled, too, though it took some effort. Her gaze fell on the cheerful hand-painted flowers bordering the walls. "Maybe I should start looking into that method, myself." She plucked a stuffed white rabbit off a gleaming white shelf and bent its long ears. "Considering how everything else I've tried so far to become a mother has been a bust."

Wendy deftly adjusted her nightgown as she shifted the baby to her shoulder. "Honestly, Em. Only you would come out of a tornado with a spreadsheet in her head that lays out every possible way to become a mommy. Did you ever consider just trying to meet a *man* first?" She patted MaryAnne's back and was quickly rewarded by a decidedly indelicate little burp. She grinned and stood up from the glider.

"You're sounding surprisingly old-fashioned. These days, I hardly need a man in my life to become a mother." Emily reached out for her niece. "Let me take her."

Wendy surrendered the baby happily enough. "Far be it for me to suggest that you won't handle being a single mother as admirably as you handle your career, but I *am* a mother now. And I'm here to tell you that I can't imagine doing this without Marcos."

Emily sighed a little. "I'm thirty years old. If there were a *Marcos* out there for me, I'd have found him by now."

Wendy lifted her eyebrows. "Really? Where? In the offices of FortuneSouth? That's pretty much where you've spent all of your time since...forever!"

"I'm not at FortuneSouth now, am I?" Emily reasoned. "And I'm not looking for romance, anyway. Romance has never led anywhere. But raising a child? That's another story. I'm *going* to be a mother. Pure and simple." Emily jig-

gled MaryAnne and smiled as her niece chortled happily. "Isn't that right, sweetie peetie?
Auntie Emily is going to get a baby."

"Romance for you has never gone anywhere
because you've never made room for it to go
anywhere."

"I've dated plenty of men!"

"Yeah. Maybe once. Twice if they were
lucky. How many have you loved more than
your job?"

Emily rolled her eyes. "None of them were
anywhere near as interesting as my job. And
most were more interested in what I could do
for them, than in what we could be together."
She grinned good-naturedly. "Besides, I figure
there are a finite number of good men out there
and you and Jordana have already snapped up
this family's allotment of them."

Wendy just shook her head and seemed
to see the wisdom in changing the subject.
"Speaking of Jordana. What time are you
going over to Tanner's office today?"

Tanner Redmond was the newest addition
to the Fortune fold, having recently married
their sister. "I said I'd be there by three. But
I'm meeting with the adoption attorney again
at eleven."

"Then before you go, I'm gonna go grab

a shower while the grabbin's good." Wendy strode out of the nursery, her scarlet nightgown flowing behind her.

Maybe Emily was the only one with spreadsheets in her head, but Wendy was the only one whose vivid personality was enough to eclipse even scarlet-colored silk. Emily held up MaryAnne until they were nose-to-nose. "Your mama sure found her place, didn't she?" There'd been times when the entire family had wondered if their wild young Wendy would ever settle anywhere.

MaryAnne kicked her bare little feet, her cheeks rounding as she opened her mouth in a gummy grin, and Emily felt such a wistful longing inside her that she could hardly bear it. She cuddled the baby close, carrying her out of the nursery. "This time next year, you'll have a new cousin," she told her niece. "And you'll be great friends and won't ever argue over who gets to play with which doll like your Auntie Jordana and I did." There was only a year separating Emily and Jordana. By the time their live-wire baby sister, Wendy, had come along several years later, they'd both been in elementary school.

Now, both Wendy and Jordana were well into making families of their own and Emily was the odd one out. "Not for long, though, right?" She jiggled MaryAnne as she walked through her sister and brother-in-law's home.

She'd been up and showered for hours already; the early-to-rise habit sticking even though she'd been away from home base in Atlanta for nearly three months now. She'd already toyed some more with the mock website that she wanted to show Tanner, dealt with a few minor crises with her staff at Fortune-South and saved a bunch of real estate listings she was interested in looking into on her cell. And as soon as Wendy was finished showering, Emily would meet with the adoption attorney she'd been working with for the past few months. If that meeting ended up as fruitless as all the others she'd already had, then she'd confirm her appointment next week with the gynecologist to go forward with a second insemination attempt. After that, she'd head out to Tanner's office for the brief duty-meeting with Tanner and his marketing guy.

She didn't particularly mind the meeting. It had sort of been her own fault, anyway, because she'd happened to mention that the website for his flight school was a little...dry. Fortunately, her new brother-in-law hadn't been offended. Instead, he'd asked her to come in and discuss the matter, as well as kick around some marketing and advertising strategies for increasing the flight school's business. Of course, she'd said she would. He was Jordana's brand-new husband and the father of the baby they were soon expecting, so how could Emily refuse?

Besides, she liked Tanner.

And even though she'd come up with the mock site herself—something she had some fun doing, even though the technical end wasn't particularly her area of expertise—it didn't mean she was particularly interested in discussing business with anyone any more than she was interested in her own duties with FortuneSouth these days.

For the first time in her life, Emily's eye was not only on business. She'd realized what mattered and one way or another, she *was* going to become a mother.

Not because she was trying to keep up with her sisters. But because it was the one thing she'd come out knowing, after that horrible day when the tornado had ripped through the Red Rock airport, seemingly bent on changing all of their lives.

She was thirty years old. She was alive. She wanted to be a mother. To give all the love inside her that she had to give to a child, the same way she'd always known her mother loved her.

And she wasn't going to waste any more time.

Max Allen eyed the plain watch on his wrist and held back an oath while he picked up his pace, crossing the tarmac from the Red Rock Regional Airport's terminal to the hangar that housed Redmond Flight School. Admittedly, he wasn't looking forward to the meeting that his boss, Tanner Redmond, had set up with his sister-in-law. But that didn't mean he wanted to be late for it.

After a month, he still had a hard time believing that he was even working for Tanner as his assistant. Which meant he also needed to swallow the obvious fact that his boss figured he needed some help and had asked him to meet with Emily Fortune.

Best thing Max could do was forget about all the reasons he wasn't qualified to handle any sort of sales and marketing for the flight school, and learn anything and everything he could from the high-powered advertising executive.

He skirted a slow-moving fuel truck, absently giving the driver, Joe, a wave, and broke into a jog to cross the last fifty yards. Not a smart move, he realized, when he pushed through the door to the business office and cool air-conditioning wafted over him, reminding him that it was a hot June afternoon out there.

Not only was he running late, but he was going to *look* like he'd been running late, too.

Through the window of Tanner's office, he could see the back of a blond head. The woman had already arrived. Naturally.

He shoved his hand through his hair and blew out a deep breath. Hell with it. The lady would just have to put up with him the way he was. Sweating, unqualified and all. Before long, Tanner would probably realize the error of his ways and Max would be out of the job, anyway.

At least he had the animals at the Double Crown where he still worked part-time as a ranch hand. They didn't have to bother seeing beyond his checkered past; all they cared about was getting their feed and water when they needed. And he was pretty sure that Lily Fortune would let him go back to full-time, even though the woman had been one of the ones to encourage Max to take a chance with the flight school gig when Tanner had offered it.

He reached out and pushed open Tanner's office door, his gaze focused on his boss's face. "Sorry I'm late." Might as well get the obvious out of the way first. "I got hung up talking to the maintenance supervisor." Though the airport was up and running again, repairs were still going on from the damage caused by the December tornado.

Tanner didn't look unduly worried. "No problem." He gestured toward the woman sitting in front of his desk. "Emily Fortune," he introduced. "This is—

"You," the woman interrupted as she rose.

Max focused on her, then, and her obvious surprise. She was stepping away from the leather chair she'd been sitting in, her hand extended toward him. She was wearing a black jacket and matching pants that only accentuated her slender figure, and her pale blond hair was pulled back in a ponytail. She looked expensively professional and even though there was no dirt covering her face and no debris tangling in her hair, the green eyes staring back at him through narrow, black-framed glasses were definitely the same ones he remembered.

He must have stuck his own hand out automatically, because her smooth, warm palm met his, her long fingers clasping his in a no-nonsense way and jolting his attention away from that mossy green.

"It *was* you at the airport that day," she was saying in a smooth voice that held a trace of a Southern drawl. "Wasn't it?"

He nodded and managed to find his voice somewhere. Even though he'd figured out that day at the airport who *she* was, he'd been hoping that she wouldn't remember him. "You look like you came through it pretty well."

She smiled a little, then looked down and he realized he was still holding her hand. He quickly let go.

"I was lucky," she said. "Just a sprained ankle."

"So, I'm guessing you two *have* met." Tanner sounded amused.

Emily looked away from Max to his boss. She'd tucked her hands in the pockets of her blazer, Max noticed, and that abrupt swell of pleasure he'd felt at first dimmed. Probably not used to touching the lower class unless she was being pulled from beneath a collapsed roof by one.

"He rescued me after the tornado," she was

telling his boss. Her gaze slid toward Max. "But we never did get around to introductions." She smiled again, and tucked-away hands or not, Max felt another jolt.

"It was the rescue workers who pulled you out," he reminded.

"Yours was the voice that kept me going," she countered. "I'll never forget it."

He didn't want her gratitude. He'd done what anyone would have done. There was no point in admitting that he hadn't forgotten it, either. If she'd been just an average girl, maybe. But she'd turned out to be a Fortune. One of the FortuneSouth Fortunes.

They had money and class and first-class educations followed by first-class careers.

Way, *way* out of his league.

So he'd stuck the moments they'd shared while she'd clung desperately to his hand and stared into his eyes while a half-dozen rescue workers lifted what seemed half a building off of her in a box and tried not to think about it. Only now, as a favor to her new brother-in-law, she was supposed to teach Max how to do his job.

He looked at his watch. "We should get to it, I guess."

Her confident smile seemed to falter a little.

She looked back at Tanner. "He's right. Time's money and all that." She pulled her hands from her pockets. "I know you didn't ask me to," she told Tanner, "but I toyed around with some website ideas. I can show you that, and then we'll take a look at the marketing materials you're using now and we can go from there."

"Actually," Tanner said, pushing back from his desk, "that all sounds great, including the website stuff, but I'm going to have to leave all that for you and Max to go over." He rounded the desk. "I'm going with Jordana to her O.B. appointment." He gestured at the small, round conference table in the corner of his room. "Make yourselves comfortable here, if you want. I know there's more room there than in Max's office." He squeezed Emily's shoulder as he passed by. "If you want a tour of the place, Max can give you one. He knows every nook and cranny around here by now. Right, Max?"

Max nodded, but as his boss left the office, he couldn't help wondering what Tanner was thinking, leaving it all in Max's lap.

"Why don't we start with the tour, then? It would help if I can get a little bit of a feel for this place." Emily was looking at him, her eyebrows lifted a little. If she had any suspicion that her expertise would be wasted on someone like Max, at least she didn't show it.

"Sure." He stepped out of her path so she could exit the office. "Do you know anything about flight schools?"

She laughed a little, and the sound seemed to send heat straight down his spine. "Not a single thing," she admitted as she walked past him. "You're the expert, here."

He grimaced. Evidently, Tanner hadn't told his sister-in-law much at all. Maybe she'd have refused to help if she knew how unqualified he was. "I've only been working for Tanner for a month," he said. There was no point in putting any varnish on it. The truth was what it was. He'd started out—officially—on a part-time basis, but just a few weeks ago, Tanner had asked if he'd be willing to take on more.

Max still had a hard time believing it.

"I don't know diddly-squat about marketing," he told her.

She stopped in her tracks and looked at him. "Tanner said you are his marketing assistant."

He hated titles. Mostly because they'd only ever pointed out that he was low-man on the totem pole, which he'd been perfectly aware of. "Assistant...whatever," he said. "The marketing stuff is just a priority right now. A long time before he actually hired me, though, I was mopping floors and cleaning toilets around this place." She might as well know that truth, too. "Did anything and everything, pretty much, in exchange for flying lessons."

Her head tilted slightly. The silky end of her ponytail slipped over her shoulder. "How'd you learn about the flight school in the first place?"

He shrugged. "Everyone around Red Rock's heard of the flight school." He had, even before the day he'd actually walked through the front door.

"But how," she pressed. "Radio spots? Signage?" A faint smile played around the corners of her lips, which only meant he was studying them too closely for politeness. "Good old word of mouth?"

"Word of mouth." He dragged his attention away from *her* mouth.

"Never underestimate the power of good word of mouth. It can make or break the success of any number of things," she said. "You're lucky, actually. You've got a unique perspective, Max."

Again, he felt heat slide down his spine. "How?"

"You've already been your own prospective customer." She turned again and headed along the tiled hallway that led from the front door of the business office to the rear that opened out into the hangar. "You know what brought you to Redmond Flight School."

He was pretty sure that "desperation" wasn't the angle that Tanner wanted them to promote. Fortunately, Emily was unaware of his thoughts as she continued.

"So now what you need to think about is what would have brought you here even more quickly." She glanced at him.

"Money." It was an obvious answer. One that hadn't exactly applied to him at the get-go but sure had ever since.

She sent him a smile over her shoulder again, obviously not shocked by his blunt tone. "Part of your job, then, is to convince the masses that money isn't the object. Learning to fly is."

"If everyone knew how it felt to be up there, we wouldn't need to advertise." He reached past her to push open the heavy metal door and got a whiff of something soft. Almost powdery.

Nothing around the hangar smelled like that, including him. Which just left her.

He would have been happy to stand there a long while breathing in that completely feminine fragrance, but she was already moving through the door, that long ponytail of hers swinging.

If he'd ever thought anything was particularly sexy about a woman's hair, it was only when it looked messed up from his hands tangling in it. But there was definitely something sexy about Emily's swinging length of sleek, corn-silk blond. He wondered what it would look like flowing over her bare shoulders.

"That's even better," she said, stopping again to turn on her heel and face him. Beyond her glasses, her eyes were animated. "You're already honing in on your messaging," she said, thankfully oblivious to his wayward mind. "Show your prospective customer what it feels like."

The palms of his hands were suddenly itching. He shoved them in the pockets of his blue jeans. "What it feels like," he repeated, feeling about as dumb as a rock.

"Up there." She waved her hand. "You said it yourself. If everyone knew how it felt to be up there." She pulled off her glasses, folded them and tucked the earpiece down the front of her jacket, giving him the briefest of glimpses of something black and lacy beneath, which did not help his distraction any.

"So…show me around," she invited. "My only contact with airports has been as a passenger."

A first-class passenger, he figured, but kept the thought to himself. Maybe if he concentrated enough on describing everything to do with the physical layout of the flight school, he'd get his thoughts off of *her* physical layout.

"This area, obviously, is the classroom." He pushed on a hidden partition halfway down the main wall. "We can break it up into three smaller classrooms with partitions like these." He nudged the partition wall and it smoothly disappeared again. "They're all new additions since the tornado. Just had the desks delivered a few days ago, in fact."

Emily wandered among the empty chairs that looked reminiscent of her high-school days, complete with an attached desktop, and wondered fleetingly what Max had been like in high school. Probably football team captain and hotly pursued by all the cheerleaders.

She had not been a cheerleader. Too ambitious with her eye already on making her place in her father's company. Hoping that then, maybe, he'd see something worthwhile in her.

She abruptly pulled her thoughts back into

the present. Ever since the tornado, she'd vowed to focus on the future. Period.

She glanced at Max and despite her good intentions, had to work hard to focus on her purpose there and not *him*.

Max had put another few chairs in between them. His eyes were still the same blue that they'd been that December day. But all of the gentleness in them that she'd clung to in those brief moments before he'd disappeared among the rescue workers crowding around her was nowhere in sight. Now, those eyes were completely unreadable.

She found him no less compelling, though.

Which was so not her purpose right now.

She mentally shook her head, trying to get her thoughts in order. It was more difficult than it should have been. "I, um, I know the terminal was badly damaged. But how much damage did Tanner's building sustain?"

"It was still standing. Barely."

She walked over to a white erase board that stood on wheels in front of the desks. "Really? I had no idea it had been that bad." She picked up one of the markers from the tray at the bottom of the board and toyed with it, wishing that her heart would stop its frantic little cha-cha inside her chest.

"The roof was gone. Half the planes had some sort of damage. The offices needed to be completely gutted and built over."

"That's a lot of repairs accomplished in a short amount of time. I'm impressed."

He shrugged. "That's Tanner."

"He is a force to be reckoned with." She smiled wryly. "Or so my sister, Jordana, says." She dropped the marker back in the tray. "Okay." She eyed the classroom's trappings. "So you have the ability for multiple classrooms. What happens in them?"

"Ground school."

"Which is…what?" She couldn't help looking at him again. He wore plain old blue jeans and a white button-down shirt incredibly— with a capital *I*—well. "You're the knowledgeable one, remember?"

"There are rules in flying just like there are rules in driving. FAA regulations. Have to learn them as well as some basic aeronautics and be able to pass a test on them. You don't learn everything in the cockpit. In fact, most of it seems like it's done sitting at a desk whether in a classroom with other students or on a one-to-one basis with a private instructor." He shrugged. "Classroom's obviously more economical for the student pilot, but we offer a lot of different options."

She propped her hip on one of the desks. "How many instructors does Tanner have?"

He looked away, but she could see the abruptly grim turn of his lips. "Eleven, now. Gary Tompkins died in the tornado. He was my first instructor."

Regret pinched hard. She'd known Tanner had lost an employee and wished that she'd shown more tact. "I'm so sorry."

"He was a good guy." His gaze slanted back at her. "As patient as the day is long, which was a good thing when it came to teaching me." She was glad to see his expression lightening as he shook his head, looking wry. "Probably telling the same old stories in heaven that he was always telling everyone down here," he said.

She smiled. "Did you always want to know how to fly?"

He shook his head, that bit of lightness in his expression fading, and leaving her wanting it back again. "That's more recent."

But he didn't elaborate, which only left her wondering about him even more.

He glanced at the sturdy leather watch strapped on his wrist and gestured toward the door opposite the one they'd come through. "Anyway, Tanner hasn't replaced Gary yet. He's interviewing now, though. But he's also interviewing for commercial pilots since he's set a July 4 launch date next month for his charter business expansion, and he wants to get another ATP on board."

"ATP?"

"Airline Transport Pilot. Highest rating you can get. Tanner has it. He wants a backup."

She wasn't surprised about Tanner's ambitious business plans. He'd received the "John Michael Fortune" seal of approval when it came to business, after all, and that wasn't an easy thing to come by. She passed through the doorway when Max pulled it open for her and nearly lost her train of thought again when her shoulder brushed against his. "Any…any other employees besides the instructors?"

"Just me." He touched the small of her back briefly, directing her toward the rear of the soaring building. Sunlight shined through the long, narrow windows set high in the rafters onto an assortment of small planes parked in precise order on the gleaming floor. The main door was open, too, and she could see the airport terminal some distance away. "Our simulator room is back here," he said.

He ushered her into another room, this one considerably smaller than the classroom, which could have easily seated a few dozen students.

This one only seemed to have room for two.

He dropped his hand on top of the enclosure that surrounded what looked—eerily, to her—like an airplane's cockpit. "One of three sim rooms," he said. "Most places just have two. And these are state-of-the-art." He kept moving, passing the doorways that obviously housed the other two flight simulators, before exiting out into the main hangar area again. "We have aircraft available for lessons as well as rentals." He waved at the planes as he walked toward the closest one. "Slow day today, though. Half the fleet is in. Usually they're all out this time of day."

Surprised, she looked over the planes again. "Where do the rest of them go?"

His eyes glinted with amusement, and she felt that strange trip inside her chest again. "They all fit," he assured. "Close as sardines, but they fit."

"I wouldn't want to have to park one," she admitted, eyeing the wingspan of the plane.

"Just takes some muscle and some careful attention. We've also got some planes outside on tie-downs." He finally stopped walking and leaned against the long tail of a white plane with a propeller on its nose. "Have you ever been up in a small plane?"

She eyed the airplane behind him. He was as tall as the top of the wing. "Depends on your definition of small." There'd been plenty of times she'd flown on a private jet for business, but it had still been a jet. Multiple engines and all. "That thing there practically looks like a toy."

"Pretty expensive toy." He glanced at the plane and she couldn't help but see the distinct fondness in his expression.

"You look at it like she's a beautiful woman."

"Well." He ran his palm along the edge the wing. His gaze, though, didn't move from her face. "She does give plenty of pleasure."

Even though she was the one to bring it up, she felt her face turn warm. And there was no point in denying it. He could see her blush just as easily as she could feel it and a faint smile flirted around the corners of his lips.

It wasn't a full-on smile, but just then it seemed wholly worth the price of her silly blush.

"All right, then." She clapped her hands together. "Maybe it's time we go to your office and we look at the marketing materials. If you want to see the mock-up I did, I can pull that up for you, as well."

His head dipped slightly in agreement. He pushed away from the plane. "That's what you're here for."

Yes. That *was* what she was there for. Help out with some advertising tips and get back to her own priorities. All she needed to do was keep herself as focused as she'd always been.

Then Max touched her arm, guiding her away from the plane.

She quickened her step toward the hangar door. But she couldn't walk fast enough to outrun the shivers flitting down her spine.

Chapter 2

"I'm serious," Emily insisted, several hours later. "There's no earthly reason why you can't learn this design program if you want to."

They'd started out at the conference table in Tanner's office, but had ended up in Max's closet-size office where she was hunched on a little stool next to his chair beside his desk. Even though his office was cramped, the computer humming on the desk in front of them was state-of-the-art.

Max just shook his head, though. Despite what she'd found to be an incredibly creative mind as they'd brainstormed various advertising themes and she'd plugged some of the ideas into the sample website, now he just seemed adamant that he couldn't also learn the graphics program that she, herself, personally favored. "Tanner's always had his brochures and stuff designed by a company that specializes in that sort of thing."

Feeling frustrated, Emily pushed her fingers through her hair, getting caught in her ponytail. She absently tugged on the band until it slid free. "That doesn't mean they have to be," she countered. She was focused on the computer screen where she'd been able to pull up her own computer at FortuneSouth over the internet, so she could show him some examples of the projects her department worked on.

She leaned closer to tap the oversize monitor screen. "This is a full-color brochure that we did a few months ago for a special corporate promotion we offered to one of Atlanta's larger construction firms. We wanted it specifically targeted to their employees. So we did a small print run that we easily handled in-house." She reached for the computer mouse, unintentionally brushing her hand against his before he quickly moved it away.

Ignoring that, as well as the way her hand tingled, she clicked a few times. Opened a second project so both were displayed. "Same exact brochure layout used again last week with redesigned messaging for a corporate law firm in Boston. Small print run again, minimal time spent revising the variables."

Max was leaning back in his chair. He'd folded his arms across his chest. "I get the advantage of it," he said. His voice was flat. "I just don't know if it's something I'm going to be able to master. I'm taking care of other stuff around here, too, that I can't ignore. And if Tanner goes for all those website ideas of yours, I'm gonna be updating that every time I turn around, too."

"We can minimize the effort of updating," she assured. "And I admit there are entire courses designed around learning this graphics software." She scraped her hair back and pushed it through the band. "But I could teach you the basics."

His lips twisted. "You got the next six months available?"

"Don't be so negative," she chided. "It'll take a few afternoons. It doesn't have to take you away, entirely, from your other duties. I've got the time if you do."

"Tanner's going to owe you big."

She sat up, stretching her back. It felt like she'd been hunched over his desk, sitting on that little stool, for hours. But as fond as she had become of Tanner, she knew she hadn't made the offer because of him.

That offer came because of Max, himself, and she wasn't going to lie to herself by pretending otherwise.

"Advertising's my business. I'm actually good at it," she said. "I enjoy it. But I usually end up spending most of my time sitting in meetings, directing everyone else's projects while they get to do the fun stuff."

His eyebrows shot up. "This is fun?"

She couldn't help but grin. She *had* enjoyed coming up with the website as a surprise for Tanner. But she focused on Max. "Don't pretend you don't have a creative bone in your body." She waved at the notes covering his desk. They contained just as many scribbles as hers. "You're able to focus on the essentials, but not get your thinking locked into a box. Not everyone can do that, you know."

Instead of smiling himself, though, he compressed his lips. He shifted and his desk chair gave a soft squeak while his gaze focused again on the computer screen. "Are you hungry?"

She blinked. "What?"

"I should've closed up shop two hours ago. It's supper time."

"Oh." Of course. Her gaze flew guiltily to the small window that was all his office possessed. The sky was nearly dark. "I'm sorry. I got caught up in what we were doing." She quickly pushed off the stool and carried it from behind his desk. He'd gotten it from the break room just down the hallway. "Of course you want to be done." How many times had her assistant, Samantha, back at FortuneSouth had to remind Emily that the employees had lives beyond the walls of the company?

"All I asked was if you were hungry," he commented before she reached the doorway.

She hesitated. "Well, I guess I am," she admitted. She hefted the stool a few inches. "I'll put this back in the break room."

"Emily—"

She stopped in her tracks again, realizing that it was the first time he'd actually spoken her name.

She liked it.

"I was thinking we could continue this over dinner."

Surprise held her still. She liked that idea, too. Probably more than she ought to, since it wasn't exactly a date. Not that she *wanted* a date.

He was interesting and attractive and smelled incredible, and if she was interested in having a date with *anyone,* Max's name would be at the top of a very short list. But the only dates she had planned in her future were those designed to put a baby in her arms.

It was pretty much a foregone conclusion that mentioning *that* plan to him would put the kibosh on him wanting to spend anything other than a business dinner with her.

"Um, okay. Sure. Unless you'd rather I just come back another day?"

He was already pushing back from his chair and gathering up the papers strewn over his desk. "Nope." He stuffed the pages into a folder and opened the top drawer of his desk to pull out a set of keys. "Just leave the stool," he said.

Feeling a little slow in the face of his sudden motion, she quickly set the stool out of the path of the doorway and grabbed her purse from where she'd left it on top of the filing cabinet that stood beneath the little window.

"Wait here while I lock up the front," he suggested. "I've got more doors to take care of out back."

In minutes, he returned and led the way back to the classrooms, checking doors and light switches as he went, plunging the hallway into darkness. "Hold on." His hand reached back when she bumped right into him.

"Sorry," she murmured.

His hand unerringly found hers. "My fault. Nearly there. Two more doors and we'll be out of here."

She opened her mouth and let out a silent breath as she followed behind him. She felt as silly as a schoolgirl with her first crush from nothing more than the heat of his fingers against hers.

Too quickly, he'd finished his rounds and they reached the back door. He let go of her hand as he pushed it open. Light from the lampposts outside flooded over them and she waited while he set the security system and locked up. "Do you have a problem with break-ins?"

"No. But Tanner doesn't take chances, either." He pocketed his keys and they walked around the building until they reached the parking area near the front of the office.

Aside from the luxury rental car that she'd had since March, the only other vehicle in the lot was a dark pickup truck.

She stopped at her car. "Shall I drive, or follow you?"

His gaze seemed to hesitate on the Mercedes. "What kind of food do you like?"

"How about Red?" Wendy's husband, Marcos, managed the popular restaurant.

He nodded and headed toward his truck. "See you there."

Which answered that, she thought, feeling a little pinch that she knew she had no business feeling. She rummaged through her purse, hunting for her key fob. She finally found it and unlocked the car, aware that Max was already in his truck and waiting. She quickly started the car and drove out of the lot, ridiculously conscious of his headlights in her rearview mirror.

By the time they made it to the restaurant and she found a parking spot in the crowded lot, she had her emotions well in hand again. She could see him driving through the lot, and she went inside to get their names on the waiting list while he hunted for his own parking spot.

"Inside, or the courtyard?" the hostess asked.

Emily peered past the people waiting to be seated. The restaurant was located in a converted hacienda and possessed an open-air courtyard in the center of the building. "Courtyard, please." The heat of the day had passed, leaving the evening temperature nearly perfect. And there were a few tables still available there.

The girl smiled and made a notation on her list before gathering a pile of menus in her hand and moving off with a well-dressed couple.

Emily went out in front again to wait for Max. He was just crossing the parking lot, his legs eating up the distance. "I requested the courtyard," she told him when he reached her. "If that's all right with you."

"It's fine." He nodded toward one of the benches situated outside. "You want to sit?"

She made a face. "Feel like my rear end is still flat from sitting too much already."

He pinched his earlobe. "Whatever I say to that is probably going to get me into trouble."

She felt her face go warm again. "I wasn't hunting for a compliment."

"I wasn't trying to look at your rear end all afternoon, either," his voice was matter-of-fact. "Some things just happen when a woman looks like you."

Her jaw loosened. She didn't know what to

say to that. So she said nothing, and the silence started to stretch awkwardly.

Max was wishing he could cut off his tongue when the hostess mercifully poked her head out the door and called their name, but the truth was already out there.

He followed Emily through the busy restaurant and couldn't help but notice that she slipped into one of the chairs at the small table they were shown to in the courtyard so quickly that he didn't even have an opportunity to pull it out for her. He took the other chair and waited until the hostess handed them their menus and departed again before opening his fool mouth again. "This is a business dinner," he said. "I shouldn't have said what I did."

There was a candle burning in the center of the intimate table and her eyes looked huge and mysterious behind the glasses she wore. "Don't worry about it." She unfolded her menu. "Considering my brother-in-law is a manager here, you'd think I'd know the menu inside and out by now but I don't." Her voice had that too-bright pitch that told him she was bugged about something.

By his inappropriate comment in the first place, or the fact that he'd apologized for it?

"What do you like here?" she asked, her gaze on her menu.

Her. He liked her.

He held back a sigh and opened his own menu. "Everything's good. You could close your eyes and point and you wouldn't be disappointed."

"Good evening." A waiter stopped next to their table, and set condensing glasses of water in front of them. "Welcome to Red. Can I start you off with a cocktail?"

"I'd love a margarita," Emily said. She pulled off her glasses and tucked them in her jacket again. "On the rocks."

"Very good. Salt?"

"Is there a point to a margarita without salt?" she returned humorously.

"Not in my estimation," the waiter allowed, grinning. He was young and good-looking and obviously didn't have a problem waiting on Emily.

Max felt an urge to punch the kid.

"And for you, sir?"

"Lemonade. Lots of ice."

The boy nodded. "I'll get those right out to you."

"Margaritas have no place in dinner meetings for you, I guess," she commented after the waiter left.

"I don't drink."

Her lips parted. She hesitated. Then she shook her head a little. "I'm sorry. I've put my foot in it, again."

He frowned and realized he'd sat forward, even though she'd leaned back in her chair. "What are you talking about?"

"I just thought maybe we could relax a little bit. I certainly don't need to have a cocktail if you're opposed to drinking for...whatever reason."

"I don't have a drinking problem," he clarified bluntly. "Not since I quit. Is that what's worrying you?"

Her head cocked. She slipped her glasses back on her nose. "I wasn't worried. I just didn't want to make you any more uncomfortable than you already seem."

"I'm not uncomfortable."

Emily eyed him, lifting an eyebrow. "Really? Smile much?"

For a beat, his handsome face looked surprised. Then his lips tilted. "Sorry. Better?"

She felt a definite dip inside her tummy at that crooked smile. "Much better." Though her pride wasn't too happy at the breathless way she sounded. She took a sip of her water, determined to follow the order of the evening. Which was business. "So, besides being tasked with the marketing materials, what else does Tanner have you doing around the school?"

Unfortunately, the question didn't seem to relax him any. "Scheduling, billing, you name it. He handles all the stuff the FAA requires, but I've got the bulk of the rest of the paperwork." He picked up his own water glass. "Lots of paperwork."

"I can imagine. What'd you do before you started working for Tanner?"

"Worked as a ranch hand. Still do on the weekend if I'm not flying."

If she hadn't seen for herself his natural abilities inside the office, she would have figured that sort of outdoor work was much more his style. "What ranch?"

"The Double Crown."

She sat back, surprised. "That's Lily and William's place."

He nodded. "You're related, right?"

"Distantly." She smiled briefly at the waiter when he set their drinks on the table. "Thanks." She touched the menu that she'd barely glanced at. "Can we have a few more minutes?"

The waiter nodded and disappeared again.

A waitress passed by carrying a heavy tray of food. Emily couldn't help noticing the way the girl's eyes fixed longingly on Max. She couldn't blame her. Emily was having a difficult time not just sitting back to admire the view, herself. He was tall—easily six feet, she'd guess—and his short brown hair was a little shaggy, but thick and glossy-looking all the same. He had an extremely masculine appearance—not fussy at all, but all the more attractive as a result. And his eyes—his eyes were as pale blue as the Red Rock summer sky.

"All the Fortunes here are cousins something-something removed," she said, hastily returning to the conversation at hand before he realized she was ogling. "But getting to know them all better has been really nice. So, you must like horses and cattle and all that?"

He shrugged. "As long as they're getting what they need, they don't care who is feeding and watering. Or shoveling." His long, blunt fingers surrounded his sweating lemonade glass.

Her gaze slid from his fingers, up along his sinewy wrist. She swallowed and quickly reached for her margarita, looking away for a quick moment toward the glistening water flowing down the tiered fountain situated in the center of the courtyard to gather herself. "Too bad more people aren't like that."

His eyebrows pulled together for a quick second, as if she'd surprised him by the comment. But all he did was unfold his menu and look down at it.

She sipped her drink, feeling the warmth of the tequila hit her throat. She shouldn't have ordered the drink. As he'd said, this was a business dinner. Add in the fact that she hadn't eaten since that morning…

She set the heavy margarita glass down and stared at her own menu. But she didn't really see the words. She was fairly certain that there'd been a board listing the chef's specials at the front of the restaurant which would make choosing easy, since she couldn't manage to concentrate on anything other than Max.

She closed her menu decisively. "Tell me a little more about how you got your pilot's license. Are you able to fly often on the weekends? Where do you go? What do you do?" She couldn't imagine when he had the time, considering he was holding down two jobs.

"I don't necessarily have places in mind to

go. It's the flying itself that grabs me. And technically, it's not called a license but a certificate," he said, closing his own menu. "Right now I'm working on my instrument rating. I put a lot of time in on the simulator. Sunday afternoons roll around and I'm either in the sim room or up in the air."

She shook her head slightly. "Frankly, I find it a little alarming that pilots learn how to fly sitting in front of a fancy computer."

His expression lightened. She'd noticed that happened whenever he talked about flying. "We have to put in that air time, as well. Only some of our hours can come from the sim. The sim's not only less expensive—no aircraft, no fuel—but sometimes it's easier to get the time on it. Because…no aircraft. Tanner's students are all jockeying for time in the planes. Scheduling is a bi—well, it's a real task. Sometimes you gotta settle for what you can get."

"I hadn't even thought about the fuel." She barely registered that she'd sat forward again, propping her chin on her hand. "Is it the same kind of gas we use in our cars?" She dipped her finger over the coarse salt lining her margarita glass and sucked it off her finger.

His gaze flicked away from her lips. He

shook his head. "Avgas. Aviation gas and nowhere near as cheap."

She couldn't help but laugh. "I guess that proves everything is relative. *I* think the price of filling my car's gas tank is ridiculous."

"Wouldn't think that would bother you."

She felt a little pause. "Because I'm a Fortune, you mean?"

He held up his lemonade glass, tilting it a little toward her as if to say "bingo."

"Just because my family has money doesn't mean I'm unaware, or uncaring, about the cost of things."

His lips twisted a little. "And the last time you didn't do something you wanted to do because you couldn't afford it?"

She let out a little sigh. All the financial advantages that she had at her disposal hadn't put a baby in her arms, yet. Hadn't gotten her even close. Her appointment with the adoption attorney that very day had simply underscored that point. There were no women around—none that they could find, anyway—who were interested in a private adoption even though Emily was offering to cover all of the mother's medical costs. The few pregnant girls who'd responded to her attorney's ad had all passed on the opportunity when they'd learned Emily was single, and planning to stay that way.

"Money doesn't buy everything." She dipped another speck of salt off the glass and touched it to her tongue. "And money or not, I think people are like your animals out at the Double Crown. Not caring how or why so much, just as long as we have what we need."

He clearly didn't believe her. "And what do *you* need?"

She opened her mouth, but no words came.

And fortunately, the waiter returned then. She ordered the first special he reeled off and she was a little surprised when Max did the same.

Somehow, she doubted his reason was the same as hers.

The waiter disappeared again and an awkward silence fell over the table. Emily couldn't quite figure out why. She'd never felt particularly tongue-tied in any business situation before. She looked around the restaurant. The flickering candles on the tables. The gurgling fountain and the Latin-flavored music. Nothing there felt businesslike. Certainly not sitting at the small table with Max, her knees only inches from his.

She suddenly didn't want a business situation. She wanted social. And that was an area in which she'd never felt particularly comfortable. Just like Wendy had accused.

The young waitress was clearing a table beside them, but her gaze kept turning to Max, and Emily leaned over the table toward him. "I think you have an admirer," she said softly, sliding her gaze to the side.

He grimaced and, surprisingly, hunched forward, as well. "That's just Ellie."

She felt breathless with their noses only inches apart above the flickering candle. "So you *do* know her."

"She's a kid."

"I think she looks pretty grown-up to me." The girl filled out the frilly, white peasant-style blouse she was wearing in a way that Emily had given up on ever achieving when she'd hit twenty. "If looks could kill, I'd be wearing a toe tag. How do you know her?"

"She used to be a cocktail waitress at one of the bars I liked to frequent."

"Why'd you quit drinking?" She knew it was none of her business, but the question popped out anyway.

"I needed to."

Which she'd assumed, but the answer still told her nothing. She took the answer as the roadblock it had probably been meant to be and propped her chin on her hand again. Another fortifying sip of her margarita had warmth sliding down her throat.

He had the most compelling eyes. She wondered fancifully what he'd say if she told him she'd thought about his eyes more than once in the days since she'd been buried in airport rubble. "What were you doing at the airport that day?"

"When the tornado hit?" He pinched his earlobe, then dropped his hand on the table. His finger grazed her elbow. But he didn't move it away and her heart gave a funny little lurch. "I'd been over at the hangar with Gary. We saw the storm rolling in." His lips compressed for a moment. "Once we realized what was happening, he told me to head over for the terminal, do what I could do to make sure people were taking shelter, while he was gonna make sure the planes were secure in the hangar." A muscle worked in his jaw. "When I got there, it was complete mayhem. I didn't even know until later that the hangar had been hit, too. Gary was hit by a collapsing beam. Damned old man never came out of a coma."

She could all-too-easily imagine sharing

Gary's tragedy. "Instead of helping me, you could have been helping him," she said softly.

But he shook his head. "That's not the way Gary would have thought."

"Is it the way you think?"

His gaze met hers. "I think some things happen for a reason," he finally said. "And I could make myself crazy trying to understand them, or I can just deal with the facts and move forward." He made a face. "Something else that Gary taught me."

She couldn't help herself. She leaned forward, covering his hand with hers. "You were close, weren't you?"

He didn't answer immediately. And when he did, his brief "Yeah" managed to convey so much more. Then he turned his wrist, flipping his hand until their palms met.

Her heart lurched even harder.

"Two Red Flame specials," the waiter announced as he balanced a tray next to the table. "Chicken breasts stuffed with asiago cheese, spinach and sun-dried tomatoes served over roasted chiles. And you know how seriously we take our chiles here. You order 'em, you're committed."

Emily sat back again as the waiter set their

plates in front of them. She wished he would have taken a little longer with the food.

Max didn't seem to show any such disappointment, though, as he dropped his napkin onto his lap and jabbed his fork into the steaming entrée.

Emily spread her own napkin on her lap and more slowly picked up her fork. The well-known reputation that Red possessed wasn't a fluke, and even though she was more interested in her dinner companion than she was in the dinner itself, the spicy aroma coming from her plate did its magic and she tucked into the meal, feeling more ravenous than she'd expected.

Two bites in though, she realized just how spicy the dish was. "Oh, my word." She gasped, grabbing her water and downing half of it. "I've burnt off the top layer of my tongue," she said when she finally set down her water.

Max was grinning. "Didn't pay enough attention to Julio's warning when he described the dish?"

"Evidently not." She realized she was grinning, too. She couldn't help it in the face of his.

"Here." He pulled the wedge of lime off the

rim of her margarita and held it up. "Suck on this."

She didn't know what possessed her.

Maybe it was the fact that her palm was still humming from the touch of his against it. Maybe it was the way his lips canted up a little higher on the right side than the left when he smiled. Or maybe it was just the balmy evening, the flickering candlelight and the tinkling sound of water from the fountain in the center of the patio.

Instead of taking the lime from him, she simply leaned forward and sank her teeth into the small wedge, closing her lips around it to suck at the tart fruit.

His pupils flared.

Time seemed to stand still.

Finally, he let go of the lime and sat back. "You want to dance?"

She slowly drew the lime from her mouth. "Okay."

And despite the fact that their plates were still steaming hot from the kitchen, he abandoned his chair and walked around to hers, pulling it away from the table.

She stood, too, and felt a shiver trickle down her spine when it seemed as if she could feel his warm breath on her neck.

Then he held out his hand.

She dropped her glasses on the table next to her plate and set her palm against his.

Chapter 3

Max had made some gigantic mistakes in his life.

But as he worked his way through the restaurant's dining room toward the intimate dance floor, he couldn't decide if he'd just made one more, or not.

The only thing he knew for sure was that he wanted Emily Fortune up close and personal.

And, whether he could figure out why or not, she seemed to be interested in the same damn thing.

Fortunately, the music wasn't anything complicated. Just a slow, Latin beat that didn't necessitate anything more involved than shuffling around between the other couples, and he turned toward Emily. She didn't hesitate, stepping closer than he'd figured she would, and linking her hands behind his neck.

It took every speck of willpower he didn't even know he had to keep from dragging her even closer.

"This is the nicest thing that's happened to me in a long time," she said.

"I find that hard to believe."

She tilted back her head and the silky ends of her ponytail tickled his hand where it rested on her back. "Why?"

"I doubt I'm your usual taste." He stepped closer, turning her slightly to avoid the older couple dancing next to them. "I'll bet you dessert that your last date was either a lawyer or a doctor." He thought for a moment. "Or maybe some Southern trust-fund son."

For a second, he thought she would be offended. At least enough to stop dancing with him and end the spectacular torture it had become the second he'd touched her. But then she lifted her mouth, reaching up to whisper near his ear. "You owe me dessert, then, Max Allen. And I like sinfully…rich…chocolate."

His fingers curled into the expensive-feeling jacket covering her back. The only thing in his blood right now was sin. And that was a helluva problem, considering Emily was not only out of his class, but she was his boss's sister-in-law. "Who was he, then?"

"Terrance Green. A stockbroker."

He gave her a look. "Same thing."

She smiled a little tauntingly. "You didn't specify. And I *am* going to collect."

"How long did you keep old Terry dancing on your string?"

She rolled her eyes and he figured it was his imagination that she looked embarrassed. "We only went out once," she said. "I accompanied him to a charity auction."

He wondered what she'd say if he told her there'd been days during his childhood when he'd pretty much *been* a charity. "Sleep with him?"

Her jaw dropped. But then she laughed. "You truly don't bother mincing words, do you?"

"So?"

"No!" She was still smiling, as if she couldn't believe he'd ask. "Do you really think I sleep with men after only one date?"

"How many does it take, then?"

She waited a beat. "Are you just gathering

information, or do you have a more personal interest?"

He tightened his arm around her back, his thigh sliding between hers as they slowly revolved around the floor. "What do you think?"

Her smile had finally died, only to be replaced by an uncertain look that didn't do a thing to alleviate the heat literally growing between them. "I think," she finally said huskily, "it bears some investigation."

"Max?" The feminine voice broke through the thick fog that seemed to enclose them in their own seductive world. "I thought that was you."

Max wanted to swear when Emily blinked and her expression cleared. He didn't stop swaying her in his arms, though, as he looked over at his sister, who was eyeing him with no small amount of surprise.

"Kirsten." His gaze took in her husband, also. "Jeremy. Didn't know you two would be here."

His sister smiled, though her eyes were plainly curious. "We could say the same. I haven't seen you out since—"

"Jeremy," Max said abruptly, not really wanting to have his sister announce in front of Emily just how long it had been since he'd been seen in public with any woman in his arms. He hadn't dated in over a year. Back when he was thinking he was heading down the "family man" path, and his life was finally on the right track.

Until it derailed.

He let go of Emily so that she could see the other couple. "I guess you two don't really need any introduction."

"I guess we don't," Emily agreed. "Jeremy, how nice to see you." Her gaze went from her cousin something-something-removed, to his wife, and she smiled wryly. "I should have connected the names." She stuck out her hand toward Kirsten. "It's good to see you again. I didn't realize Max was your brother."

Max suddenly felt like the odd man out. His sister was married to a Fortune and Emily was born a Fortune. While he was a guy just trying to make a place for himself in the world. "Our meal is probably getting cold," he said.

"Why don't you join us," Emily suggested to his sister and her husband. "I'd love to get caught up, and we already have a table out in the courtyard."

A table that only sat two people, and closely at that.

Max managed a smile, anyway. He and his

sister had had their moments in the past, but she was his only family. He knew he could count on her, and more times than he wanted to admit, he'd had that point proven to him. She'd been the terminally responsible Allen, and for the past few years, he'd been working damn hard to prove to her—as well as himself—that he wasn't the terminally irresponsible Allen. He loved her. And he respected Jeremy a hell of a lot. Both he and Kirsten had been there for him when he'd been at his lowest point.

He just didn't want to share Emily with them at that particular moment.

"We'd love to," Kirsten assured. Her hand was tucked around Jeremy's arm.

And that was the end of that.

They headed back to their table, Emily chattering away easily with her something-removed cousin as they caught up with the family members they had in common, and the waiter managed to squeeze in two more chairs and place settings at their minuscule table.

She didn't seem to show any remorse at all that she'd invited an interruption to their privacy. Which left Max figuring that she'd wanted an interruption.

Certainly wouldn't be the first time he'd

misread a woman, but usually—when it came to the physical matters—he wasn't so far off the mark. It was just when it came to their emotions and honesty that he'd had a problem.

He ate his food, not really tasting any of it anymore. He guessed he smiled when he was meant to smile, and responded when he needed to smile, because by the time they'd finished eating and Jeremy slid his bank card to the waiter before Max could even get his hands on the check, not even Max's sister was giving him any more curious looks.

"Here." He pulled several twenties out of his wallet and tossed them on the table next to his brother-in-law's elbow.

He saw Jeremy start to wave away the money, but Max gave him a hard stare. Jeremy was an orthopedic surgeon and a Fortune. He could buy and sell Max dozens of times over. But Max paid his own way now.

Fortunately, his brother-in-law seemed to take the unspoken hint and pocketed the cash along with his credit card when the waiter returned it.

There wasn't even any need for him to hang around. Emily had her own car. And she and his sister were talking a mile a minute as if they were long-lost friends. Max caught snippets of their conversation. Talking and laughing about college and graduate degrees.

"Think I'll call it a night," he said abruptly.

The colored lights hanging around the courtyard reflected softly in Emily's glasses when she turned toward him. It was only his own wishful thinking that she seemed to show some disappointment. "Do you want to set up a time now for me to meet with you again at the office, or should I call you in the morning? The only thing I have on my schedule is a conference call, but I'll be finished with that by ten."

"Call." He realized how terse he sounded. "I don't know what's on my schedule from Tanner for tomorrow yet," he added.

Her soft lips pressed together a little, but she smiled and nodded. "Okay. Thanks for dinner."

"Sure." Before she could say anything else, he leaned over and gave his sister a kiss on the cheek. He didn't even consider a kiss for Emily—on her cheek or elsewhere. Not in front of his sister. Not when he'd already overstepped the lines of "business."

He just gave a general wave meant to cover the whole table. "See y'all later." And then he headed out of the restaurant.

* * *

Emily chewed the inside of her cheek, watching Max stride out of the courtyard. She suddenly dropped her napkin on the table. "Would you excuse me, too?" she said quickly to her cousin and his pretty wife. "I forgot to mention something to Max."

"We'll see each other again soon," Jeremy said easily. Kirsten was nodding.

Emily smiled hurriedly and grabbed her purse before quickly following the path that Max had taken. When she reached the parking lot, she spotted him already at his truck and she broke into a trot to catch up to him. "Max," she called as he unlocked his door. "Would you wait a minute?"

He turned to wait.

She felt breathless when she reached him and knew it wasn't owed entirely from her sprint across the parking lot. But now that she'd caught up to him, she felt completely tongue-tied. "Thanks for dinner."

"You already thanked me."

"I know, but… I—" She broke off, shaking her head a little. "I just really enjoyed myself."

"Catching up with your cousin?"

"No." Seemingly of its own accord, her fingers touched his arm. Which was strange, because she wasn't generally a touchy sort of person. "Well, yes, I mean it *was* good to see Jeremy. Of course. And your sister. She and Jeremy seem so perfect for each other. I meant I really enjoyed dinner with *you*."

His right eyebrow lifted slightly. "You were pretty quick to add more company."

Her lips parted. "She's your sister. How could we not invite them to sit with us? Would you rather have had me be rude?"

"I'd rather have had you to myself," he said bluntly.

That dark and sensual something that had wakened while they'd danced reared again, clenching hard inside her belly. "I'd have liked that, too," she admitted and gave a little blessing to that margarita or she'd never have had the guts to say the words aloud. "Maybe we could do this again," she added boldly. "Have dinner. Just…just the two of us."

The parking lot was too dark for her to see the expression in his eyes. "Maybe."

Maybe was just another word for *no*.

She swallowed hard and while she still had some nerve, leaned up and pressed her lips to his cheek. "That's for being there after the tornado that day," she said when she went back down on her heels.

He watched her for a moment that was so tight she felt almost sure that he was going to kiss her back.

Really kiss her.

But he didn't. He just nodded and pulled open his truck door. "You know your way back to your sister's from here?"

"Yes."

"Drive carefully."

"You do the same." Her voice was faint.

He started up the truck engine and she backed away several feet and watched him drive away.

She wasn't sure what had just happened.

All she knew was that she felt shaky.

And ridiculously disappointed.

"You were out late last night."

Emily looked up from the coffee she was pouring into a mug when Wendy padded silently into the kitchen the next morning. "Not terribly."

"It was practically ten." Wendy reached around her for a coffee mug of her own. "What were you doing?"

Mildly amused, Emily filled her sister's mug and replaced the pot on the coffeemaker's burner. "Maybe I was going wild and crazy like my little sister used to do."

Wendy made a face. "Ha-ha. Your idea of wild and crazy is leaving the house without a bra on under your tailored shirt." She twisted her hair up in a deft twist and stuck a clip in it that she pulled out of the pocket of her silky red robe. Then she poured some cream into her coffee and carried it over to the kitchen table that sat in a sunny little alcove. She sank down onto a chair and stretched out her long, shapely legs before sipping her coffee with cat-like pleasure.

Emily just shook her head. Her sister could roll out of bed and look like a magazine spread for lingerie. She, though, would have to fuss with her hair for two hours just to get some semblance of style into the stubbornly straight strands and she'd have had to have some serious surgery to gain some of the curves that Wendy came by naturally.

And sad to say, Wendy had her pegged when it came to the whole "wild and crazy" thing.

"You're the kind of woman who makes women like me feel like dish rags," she muttered.

Wendy rolled her eyes. "So says the epitome of strikingly beautiful Nordic blondes," she returned. "I know why *I'm* feeling sleepy this morning. Because my beautiful daughter woke up twice last night. But what's got you so cranky this lovely morning? Anything to do with whatever mischief you were getting up to last night?"

"I'm not cranky. And there was no mischief. I had dinner with Max Allen." Emily sat down across from her sister and sank her nose into her coffee mug. "This decaf stuff is for the birds." She got back up and added a hefty dose of cream to it.

"Not cranky my hind end," Wendy observed. "Open up that plastic container there next to the stove. Maybe you'll find something in there that'll help."

Emily opened the container and stared almost lasciviously at the pastries inside. "Did you make these?"

"I did."

She plucked one flaky croissant-shaped item out of the container and set it on a paper napkin. "I still can't believe you can cook."

Wendy laughed. "Baking isn't cooking," she said.

"It's harder," Marcos said, entering the kitchen just then. He leaned over his wife, planting a kiss on her lips that seemed to raise the temperature in the room by a good five degrees.

Emily just focused on her flaky pastry that tasted a little like almonds and a lot like something sinful. She couldn't very well tell her brother-in-law and sister to "get a room" when they were right in their very own home.

Emily was the interloper here.

She took another huge bite of the pastry and added a spoon of sugar to her coffee. Maybe if she went into a sugar coma, she'd be able to forget about the way she'd practically thrown herself at Max the evening before. "I'm going to take a shower," she said to nobody in particular, before leaving the room with her creamy, sweet coffee and a second pastry.

"What's eating her?" she heard Marcos ask.

She reached the guestroom she'd commandeered before she heard her sister's reply. But if she'd thought she'd avoid her sister's curiosity entirely, she was wrong, which she learned when Wendy boldly walked into the bathroom a while later while hot water poured down on Emily's head.

"So…" Wendy flipped down the lid on the commode, blithely ignoring the glare that Emily gave her from around the shower curtain, "Max Allen?"

"It was business," Emily said shortly, yanking the shower curtain back in place and sticking her face into the spray of water.

"Until ten o'clock business?"

Emily turned her back to the water and rinsed the shampoo out of her hair. "You knew I was meeting with him for Tanner."

"And again...until ten o'clock?" Wendy's voice was full of laughter.

Emily yanked the curtain back enough to eye her sister. "It was just business."

"Methinks you sound a little defensive, sister dear."

Emily shut off the water and stuck her hand out. "Make yourself useful and hand me a towel."

Wendy dutifully pressed a fluffy white towel into her hand. Emily swiped it over herself and wrapped it around her torso before fully pulling back the shower curtain and stepping out. "We had a lot to go over," she said. She found a comb in her toiletry bag and began dragging it through the tangles in her hair. "So we worked through dinner at Red."

"My favorite restaurant," Wendy inserted, grinning. "For obvious reasons." Not only did Marcos manage the place, but Wendy was the pastry chef there. "And very romantic."

Emily ignored that. "Excellent food was the goal. But we did run into Jeremy and Max's sister, Kirsten, there." She slid a glance toward her sister. "Why didn't you remind me that Max was her brother?"

Wendy shrugged. "I didn't think about it, to be perfectly honest. Why is it a big deal?" Her gaze was still sharp. "I mean, since your interest in Max is just business, anyway?"

Emily slapped her comb down on the vanity before she tore out her hair by the roots and picked up a tube of face cream instead. "I just felt sort of like an idiot." She squeezed out a few drops of cream and worked it in. "He's practically a relation."

Wendy picked up the tube that Emily had set down and took the top off, smelling it. "Hardly. Jeremy Fortune is a distant cousin which means his brother-in-law is perfectly free game for an interested woman."

Emily exhaled noisily. "Wendy, I am *not* interested that way."

"Lies'll give you wrinkles," Wendy advised. She held up the expensive cream. "Better use a little more of this."

Emily snatched the tube out of her sister's hand and capped it again. Then all of her irritation seemed to fizzle out of her. She stared at herself in the mirror but was only seeing Max in her mind's eye. "Do you know much about him?"

"Some." Wendy picked up the comb and stood behind Emily. "Don't you have conditioner or something to keep your hair from tangling like this?"

"I'm out. Please don't tell me you dated him, too." Until she'd fallen for Marcos, Wendy had been quite the social butterfly.

Wendy tsked and started working gently at the snarls. "I never dated Max Allen," she assured. "I do know that he's sown some of his own wild oats, though. But then, after all that mess with little Anthony—" She broke off, shaking her head.

Emily studied her sister's reflection in the mirror over the sink. "Who's Anthony?"

Wendy's gaze met hers in the mirror. "He was Max's baby. At least that's what everyone thought for a while."

Wendy couldn't have shocked her more if she'd tried. "Max has a child?"

Wendy shook her head. "No. It's a long story. But you remember when William and Lily were supposed to have gotten married last year?"

Emily nodded. She'd heard the story more

than once about how William had gone missing on his and Lily's wedding day. All of William's sons—Jeremy being one of them—had been frantic to find him. But it had been months before he'd been found, recovering from an automobile accident, and a while after that before his memories of Lily and his family had fully returned to him.

"Well, while everyone was worrying over why William hadn't shown up at the church that day, an old girlfriend of Max's had basically dumped a baby on him, telling him it was his. He was living with Kirsten at the time and she helped him take care of the baby for a while. But the baby wasn't Max's. It was Cooper Fortune's—did you ever meet Cindy Fortune?" Wendy shook her head before Emily could answer. "Coop's mother. Anyway, it turned out that the baby had actually been left at the church the day of the wedding."

Emily turned around, staring at her sister. "Someone abandoned a baby at the church?"

"The baby's real mother. Presumably she'd done it to get the baby to his father, but that got all messed up. Obviously. And Max's old girlfriend Courtney somehow ended up with the baby, claiming it was hers and Max's. All lies, of course, and Max ended up turning the baby over to the authorities, and eventually they were able to determine that Cooper was the baby's natural father."

"So what happened to Anthony's mother?"

"It was finally discovered that she'd been driving the other car in the same automobile accident that William was involved in on his wedding day." Wendy's lips twisted sadly. "She died."

Emily was horrified. "How long did Max have the baby?"

"From what I understand, long enough to get attached. Lily told me that he makes himself scarce whenever Coop or his wife, Kelsey, are around the ranch with his son. She says that Max hasn't seen the baby since he gave him up. Says he doesn't want Anthony to be confused about who his father is. She's tried to convince Max he doesn't have to worry about that anymore, but he won't even discuss it." Wendy handed Emily the comb. "It's been over a year now."

Emily closed her fingers around the comb, the tines digging into her palm. "Maybe he's just glad to have dodged the fatherhood bullet."

Wendy shrugged. "Maybe. Personally, I don't have any idea. I just know what Lily's take of the situation is. And, I'm pretty sure Max hasn't been seeing anyone since. So the field is clear for you if you're interested."

For a woman who'd never factored romance in her life, Emily didn't want to admit *how* interested. "It's just business between us," she said again.

Wendy just rolled her eyes and shook her head. "Stock up on that eye cream," she suggested again, before leaving the bathroom.

Alone once more, Emily turned to look at herself in the mirror. She was thirty years old. She wanted a baby…by just about any legal means that she could get one.

But entertaining thoughts about Max *and* babies in the same sentence was just purely dangerous. Particularly if Max was still hurting after giving up little Anthony.

She wouldn't use the attraction between them just to see her own needs fulfilled.

Would she?

Chapter 4

Emily was no closer to an answer later that day when she visited Tanner's office again to meet with Max.

She'd called him that morning to check what time was best for him and there'd been nothing remotely personal in his response. And as she sat beside him, giving him a basic tutorial of the graphics program she preferred, she couldn't help wondering all over again if she'd blown up the attraction between them in her mind. A result of her own desire for a family of her own?

"How's that look?"

She gathered her wandering thoughts and

focused on Max's brochure layout showing on the computer screen. "It looks great." And then she focused a little harder. "Really, *really* great." His design was eye-catching, modern and simple. And he'd picked up most of the basics in the span of an afternoon. "I don't have people in my department who pick up things as quickly as you do."

He gave her a sideways look. "Offering me a job?"

She ignored the tightening inside her chest. "Interested in exchanging Red Rock for Atlanta?"

His lips tilted a little. He shook his head. "Once Red Rock's in your blood, it tends to stay there."

"I'm learning that myself." And then, because he was still looking at her and she was in danger of squirming in her chair, she leaned forward, tapping the edge of the layout with her fingernail. "Try offsetting the edge of the plane just a little so it looks like it's flying onto the page."

His hand covered the computer mouse again and his arm brushed against her. Emily inhaled silently and leaned back again while he moved the image.

"Nice. Looks better." He hit the print command and turned his chair until he was facing her. "I set up a lesson for you."

It was difficult concentrating when he focused those blue eyes on her. "What kind of lesson?"

His smile widened a little. "Flying."

Duh. She felt her face flush. "Right. That's not really necessary."

"Are you afraid?"

She lifted her eyebrows. "Of course not."

"Then…what's a little lesson?" His lips tilted. "It'll give you a better sense of what I need to convey with—" he reached behind him and lifted the page off the printer behind him "—stuff like this."

She slid the page from his fingers and spread it on his desk, studying it. "You're conveying quite nicely all on your own, here."

"Aren't you the least bit curious?"

She glanced at him, but her eyes seemed to hesitate on the curve of his lower lip. Very curious. "Maybe," she said much more moderately. "A little."

"All right then. Day after tomorrow. 9:00 a.m. Does that work for you?"

She had another conference call to take care of, but she could reschedule it. Her father would have a fit, but what else was new?

"Sure. Who's taking me up?" She knew it wouldn't be Max since he wasn't an instructor.

"Ross. He's good. I've flown with him several times."

"Have you ever thought about becoming an instructor?"

"Thought about it and then stopped thinking about it." He swiveled around to face his computer again and covered the mouse with his hand. "Need a commercial rating first and that alone is a lot of hours and money into the future. Not to mention having to pass the exams."

"But if that's a future you want, it *is* worth thinking about. Planning for. When that tornado hit, one of the only things I could think about was the future. Not having one."

"Fortunately, that's not the case for you." He jerked his chin toward the computer screen. "Right now I'm doing well just keeping up with this stuff. Tanner said he wants something aimed at the high school. They already offer an aeronautics class."

"So, something age-appropriate for highschoolers." Emily pursed her lips. "You might want to talk to Tanner about doing more social media for that. You know. Facebook. Twitter. Blogging, that sort of thing."

"Great. More stuff to learn."

"It's not that difficult, believe me. And we can tie it all in with the website. Even the existing site. I'm just not sure a brochure is the way to go, necessarily. Not these days. High school was a long time ago for me."

"Yeah, what? Five, six years?"

She laughed ruefully. "Hardly. Try doubling that." She studied his sharply defined profile. "When did you graduate high school?"

"I didn't." He didn't even glance at her. "GED. No Ivy League colleges for me, either."

She absorbed that. She'd already selected a sperm donor, who'd listed an Ivy League background just like hers as well as a laundry list of other qualities she'd thought would be even more advantageous to add to the gene pool. "Ivy Leagues aren't everything, either, despite what their alumni might say."

He gave her a look. "It's a lot. You want your children going to college, don't you?"

"If I ever manage to have any." The admission popped out before she could stop it. And then, because she knew too much about his situation with little Anthony—and the information had *not* come from him—she shied away from the subject. She pointed at the screen. "But if Tanner wants a print piece for the high school, we'll give him one. Go ahead and save that file with a new name—whatever's appropriate. We'll start with this as a base and modify as we go along. Maybe come up with some ideas for an online presence, as well."

And so it went. Through the rest of the afternoon, Emily and Max went from one project to another, sometimes getting close enough to a product that Max was satisfied enough with to take to Tanner for final approval, and sometimes not. They were squabbling over the wording for the high school piece when an attractive brunette stopped in Max's doorway.

Her gaze barely took in Emily as she smiled brilliantly at Max. "You going to be ready to go soon?"

Max looked at the watch strapped around his sinewy wrist. "Yeah. In a few."

"Don't disappoint me, now," the woman practically purred.

"Have I ever?" Max asked.

Emily held back a grimace and focused on the layout draft lying on the desk in front of her. Fortunately, the woman didn't hang around long after a throaty "can't wait" and disappeared again.

"It is getting late," she said. "You've caught on even more quickly than I figured you would, and you probably prefer working without someone looking over your shoulder." She reached for her purse that she'd stowed once again on top of the filing cabinet. "I know I do. If you have any questions or want to brainstorm or…or whatever…you can call me any time." She was afraid of sounding as come-hither as the brunette.

"You don't have to race off just yet."

"You don't want to disappoint—" she gestured toward the empty doorway "—your friend."

"Brandi?" His eyes narrowed a little. "She's one of the instructors. I've got a lesson scheduled with her in an hour."

"Oh." Emily was a little nonplussed. "She seemed very…friendly."

His lips tilted slightly. "Brandi's married. Just had a baby a few months ago."

Of course she did. Everyone was having babies. Except her. But at least Emily had no reason to be envious of Brunette-Brandi's relationship with Max. "If you're going flying, it's no wonder you're anxious to finish for the day." She started for the door. "I have a few things on my schedule tomorrow, but like I said, call me if you have any questions."

"I do have a question."

She hesitated in the doorway, looking back. "What's that?"

"Do you want to have dinner? Friday night?"

All the work that she'd done that day keeping her nerves on ice went right out the window.

Friday night dinners weren't about business.

He was asking her out on a date.

Maybe hadn't meant *no,* after all.

Her mouth felt dry and her heart chugged unevenly. "I can't," she said with real regret. "I have to fly back to Atlanta the day after tomorrow for some meetings on Friday. Fortune-South is set to take over another company and there are some things that I can't take care of long-distance."

"Are you going back for good?"

"No." She shook her head quickly. "Not at all." She knew that was her father's plan, but it certainly wasn't hers. "I've gone back several times already to handle one thing or another. Usually make at least one trip a month. Sometimes two or three."

"Hell of a commute."

"Most of the time I can telecommute, fortunately. But in this instance I'll be back sometime next week. Tuesday, Wednesday at the latest. And I shouldn't have to leave again for about three weeks."

"Then what about next Friday?"

She nodded. Smiled, and was embarrassingly aware that it was decidedly shaky. "I'd like that."

His eyes darkened a little. "And I'll see you tomorrow morning. Before you go up."

The flight lesson he'd scheduled. She'd nearly forgotten. The prospect of having dinner with him was consuming enough to push nearly everything else out of her head. "Right. Anything I should do to prepare?"

"Just be ready to have the best experience of your life."

Emily's smile felt even shakier.

He could have been referring to either the flight lesson or the date. Of course, he meant the flying, though. Her common sense told her that. "Sounds good to me." And then, because she could have stood there in the doorway for a long time just looking at him, she forced herself to turn around and walk away.

Max loved flying. He could look out the window, see the patchwork ground so far below, and forget all of the mistakes he'd made in his life walking that ground. He didn't think about the father who'd walked out on them when he was a kid. He didn't think about the times when their mother had wondered where their next meal would come from. He didn't think about the struggles he'd had just to get through a day of school. The failures, the insecurities, the scrabbling just to get by...it all disappeared.

Skimming through the sky, wings slicing through cottony wisps of cloud, anything seemed possible.

Brandi sat beside him, the headphones on her head allowing them to communicate more easily. She was admittedly a pretty woman. But Max's only interest in her stemmed from what he could learn from her about flying.

Emily had definitely shown some jealousy, though.

He checked the gauges in front of him. Airspeed. Attitude. Altimeter. He was flying instrument only—using only the gauges as reference to maneuver the plane, rather than his own view outside the window which was currently inhibited by the special goggles he was wearing—and all looked good. "What's your favorite restaurant?"

"Red. I love their monster margaritas, but their desserts are even better. Why?"

"Just looking for a new place to eat." He'd already been to Red with Emily. It was a great restaurant. It just wasn't what he had in mind. And as had been proven already, it was too easy to get interrupted by people they knew. "What about in San Antonio?"

"Etienne's," she said promptly. "Fabulous duck and then this one chocolate dessert that's to die for. David takes me there every year for our wedding anniversary. It's not too far from the River Walk. Parking's a pain, and the waiters are stuffy, but the food is *très magnifique*. You trying to impress a new girl?"

Emily was no girl. She was a beautiful woman. She outclassed him, out-educated him, out-everything'd him. The only thing he was, was out of his mind even thinking he had a chance with her.

But he couldn't get the feel of her off his hands. Couldn't get the scent of her hair out of his head. And the next time her lips were against him, he wanted more than just a peck on his cheek. "Something like that."

"Etienne's a place to impress," Brandi assured. "But it's not cheap. Go with your pockets loaded. That's what David says every time we go." She was silent for a moment. "Storm clouds are building to the west. Wonder if we'll get a little rain out of them this time?" She gestured at the gauges. "Go ahead and line up for your approach, and we'll hit the books for an hour before calling it a day."

Max went through the motions, thumbing the mic to communicate with the tower, and soon he set the plane on the ground.

"Perfect," Brandi praised when the plane finally came to a stop.

For the first time since he'd started flying, though, Max's mind wasn't on reviewing every aspect of the flight.

It was on Emily.

And the chocolate dessert he still owed her.

Emily stared out the window the next morning. She was more dismayed than she'd expected.

Thunder. Lightning. And pouring buckets of rain.

"If it clears up later this afternoon, Ross can still take you up," Max was saying through the phone she was holding at her ear.

"I can't this afternoon," she told him. "I promised my sister I'd babysit MaryAnne so Wendy can run over to San Antonio for an appointment." Which meant that unless Max asked her for more help, she had no reason to see him before she left town.

"No problem," he said easily. If he was disappointed, too, he hid it well. "There'll be other opportunities. Have a safe trip home."

No mention of their Friday night date. "I'll see you when I get back?" She hated the question in her tone—she feared it made her sound desperate—but couldn't help it.

"Definitely. Hope you like French food," he said.

She preferred Mexican, but it was the company she was looking forward to, not the cuisine. "I do."

"If I don't talk to you beforehand, I'll pick you up at your sister's at seven."

"Perfect. And, um, don't forget. If you want to talk advertising or about the website, anything, just say the word."

"I will."

Emily heard the click of the line as he hung up. She sighed, and held her phone to her chest.

"That sounded suspiciously longing," Wendy said.

Emily turned and looked at her sister. "It's raining."

Wendy's eyebrows rose. "I noticed. I love the rain." Then her brows lowered again and her eyes danced merrily. "Oh, right. No flying lesson, I guess. Or is it no Max this morning that has you sighing like that?"

"It's crazy." Emily flipped the slender phone end over end between her fingers. "Max isn't part of my plan."

"Your mommy project, you mean?" Wendy looked amused. "Who says that he can't be part of it?"

"I don't want a boyfriend."

"What about a husband?"

"Please." The idea shocked her. "Marriage has never been one of my life's goals."

"To our mother's dismay." Wendy threw herself down on the couch and stretched her arms above her head. "You were all about a career with FortuneSouth and getting dear old Dad's approval."

"He asked me out on a date," she said.

Wendy's eyebrows shot up. "Dad?"

"*Max*. Next Friday."

"So all of that 'just business' crap was just that? Crap?" Wendy looked positively gleeful. "I knew you were lying yesterday." She rubbed her hands together. "I love being right."

Emily picked up a decorative pillow from the chair beside her and threw it at her sister's face.

Wendy just laughed and caught it. "Emily and Max are sitting in a tree," she chanted, "k-i-s-s-i-n-g."

"What are you? Ten years old?"

"You saying you don't want any kissing where Max is concerned?" Wendy sat forward. "It's not a crime to want to sleep with a guy," she said conspiratorially.

"I know that."

"Really? When was the last time?"

"Wendy!"

"Come on. We're sisters. You can tell me."

"Five years ago."

Wendy's jaw dropped. "No way! That practically makes you a virgin all over again."

Emily grimaced. "I knew I shouldn't have told you." The truth was, her sister undoubtedly had more experience with such matters than Emily did.

"Who was it?"

"Oh, for heaven's sake. What does it matter?" She sighed noisily. "Tommy Black."

"Wasn't he one of Dad's assistants?"

"Briefly." Tommy's tenure at FortuneSouth had been terminally brief. As brief as his and Emily's two-date fling.

"No fireworks?"

Certainly not with Tommy. Or with Stewart,

who'd been several years before that. "Fireworks are overrated," she dismissed.

"So says a woman who hasn't had any," Wendy assessed. "Or you'd never make *that* statement again."

"Not everything's about sex."

"Again...so says the woman who isn't having any. Maybe Max'll be the one to light a fuse or two. Or four or five."

Emily could feel her face getting hot. She picked up a second pillow and threw it, too. Her aim was slightly better, catching her sister in the head. "I'm just having dinner with the man."

"Loosen up. Dinner can lead to dessert." Wendy clutched the pillow to her chest. "And yummy...yummy dessert. Aren't you thinking about it just the teensiest bit?"

Thinking about it. Dreaming about it. *"No."*

"Liar. You're a normal woman and you haven't had any in five years. You're thinking about it, big-time."

"Then why'd you ask?"

"Because it kills me that you're pretending otherwise! There's no shame in wanting the weight of a man on you, Em. That's generally the way *most* women get babies in their lives. And believe me, once you're pregnant, you'll realize the fireworks that came before were nothing. Marcos could be talking about a food service order, be two rooms away, and I'd want to be hanging from the chandelier having hot, monkey sex with him."

Emily winced, blotting out the image. "I'm not planning to use Max for stud service."

"You sure? You've made no secret how determined you are to have a baby of your own and I've never once seen you not bring one of your famous plans to fruition."

"Yes." She realized as she said it that she *was* sure. And it relieved her no end. "I wouldn't do that to him. And I already have another artificial insemination scheduled, anyway." All she had to do was wait until she was ovulating.

"So you're *not* going to sleep with Max."

"I didn't say that." She regretted the admission as soon as the words escaped.

"Thank goodness," Wendy declared. "Now I know you are human like the rest of us."

"Of course I'm human!"

"Emily. I love you, I really do. But the Ms. Perfect thing you've got down pat is a little intimidating."

"I'm not remotely perfect."

Wendy hooked her arm around Emily's shoulder and gave her a smacking kiss on the cheek. "I know that now. And it makes you ever so much more fun. Now, come on. I need coffee before MaryAnn wakes up again."

Emily was taking a charter out of Red Rock back to Atlanta. Max knew it, because he'd made a point of finding out. Just as he made a point of being over in the terminal when she was scheduled to be there.

He'd already seen her pilots heading toward the gate, the flight attendant hurrying to keep up with them, and figured they'd be wheels-up within minutes of Emily arriving.

Which didn't give them much time.

He'd been waiting about twenty minutes when he spotted her striding up the corridor that—six months earlier—had been torn to pieces by the tornado and wondered if she was thinking about that day or if her mind was already on the business waiting for her in Atlanta.

She definitely looked in her usual business mode, wearing a slim-fitting black suit with her blond hair pulled back in that same smooth ponytail at the back of her head. She had a caramel-colored briefcase hanging off one shoulder and was talking on her cell phone, her skinny, black-framed glasses hovering low on her narrow nose.

She'd probably be shocked silly if she knew just how sexy she looked.

And then she spotted Max and came to a dead stop.

She nudged her glasses up with one finger, said a few more words into the phone and then slid it into a pocket on her briefcase, slowly closing the distance between them. A faint smile hovered around her lips. "This is a nice surprise," she greeted.

"I was in the area," he said dryly.

Her smile widened a little. "How're the brochures coming?"

"Tanner approved the first one that we'll include in the Sunday newspaper."

"Excellent." She looked genuinely pleased.

"He had a few comments on the high-schooler one. Thinks you're probably right about the social media aspect. When you get back, if you're still interested, we can kick that one around a little more. Start thinking about revamping the website with some of your suggestions."

"Excellent." She hitched the strap of her briefcase higher on her shoulder. Her gaze went to the wall of windows that overlooked the tarmac were the planes were parked. "Can't believe it's still raining."

"Me, either. But we need the water."

"Can you fly in the rain?"

He nodded. "Long as it's not a bad storm. Good instrument practice."

"With Brandi?"

He nodded again. "She's got the most open schedule. Some folks don't think a woman is the best instructor. Especially a young, attractive woman."

Her lips thinned, obviously peeved at the slight against a fellow member of her gender. "That's ridiculous."

"I've always thought so." He lifted the briefcase strap off her shoulder, surprised by the weight of it. "Carrying rocks?"

"Feels like it. Laptop and files, I'm afraid. The people at security went through it all with a fine-tooth comb. Twice." She flicked her finger against the badge that hung from a lanyard around his neck. "Does this thing get you around all that?"

He shook his head. "Every time I come back to the gate area, I have to go through the check just like the passengers do. Gets to be a pain, but some things are worth it."

"Safety is pretty important."

"I wasn't talking about safety," he said pointedly.

Her lashes swept down. Color bloomed on her high cheekbones. "I think there's a compliment in there somewhere."

"Just speaking the truth."

She looked up at him, her eyes behind her glasses looking as vivid and sparkling as the peridot ring his family had buried his mother with. "I don't quite know what to make of you, Max Allen."

He grimaced. "I'm about as uncomplicated as it gets."

She slowly shook her head. "Too many layers to be uncomplicated." She grabbed his wrist suddenly and lifted it, angling her head to see his watch. "My charter was scheduled to leave a few minutes ago." But she didn't let go of his wrist.

"The advantage of a charter flight is that it's designed around the needs of its passengers."

"Passenger," she said. "Just me, today."

"Get lonely?"

"Not while I'm thinking about you." She shook her head, looking away. "The things I say where you're concerned. It's like my filter of propriety goes completely out the window."

He twisted his wrist until his fingers threaded through hers and he pressed his palm against hers, feeling heat stream through his veins. She wore a brilliant white blouse beneath the black suit and his gaze strayed to the sexy hollow at the base of her neck revealed by the unbuttoned collar. "There's not a lot of propriety where my thoughts about you are concerned, either."

She swallowed and he dragged his eyes upward, seeing her pupils dilate. "Max—"

"Ms. Fortune?" The flight attendant that Max had noticed earlier stopped next to Emily. She wore a discreet name badge. "We're ready for you to board, ma'am."

Emily's gaze didn't stray from Max. "I'll be right there, Sandy. Thank you."

Sandy smiled and smartly disappeared.

Max kissed Emily's knuckles and let go of her hand, stepping away before he did something really stupid, like yanking her into his arms and planting his mouth on hers. He held up her briefcase by the strap. "Think about that dessert I owe you."

Her fingers brushed against his as she took the strap. She sucked in her lower lip for a second, leaving it wet and shining. "Dessert." She nodded. "I will." And then she turned and followed the flight attendant.

Max could have sworn he heard her add "and fireworks" as she went.

Chapter 5

"Okay, Emily. You did great." Dr. Grace, Emily's Red Rock gynecologist, draped the paperlike blanket back over Emily's legs before rolling back on her little padded stool. She peeled off her gloves and made a notation on the medical chart opened on the counter next to the examining table where Emily was currently lying, her heels inelegantly propped in the stirrups. "You know the routine. Just close your eyes and relax for a while and think happy thoughts about becoming pregnant. Then come back in a few weeks for a pregnancy test if you haven't gotten your period."

"I really have to wait that long?"

Dr. Grace gave her a sympathetic look. "I told you last time that we can do a blood test as early as a week from possible conception, but the chances of a false result increase. It's up to you, though."

Emily smiled nervously. "Two weeks, then." She didn't want to have to deal with false anything. "Do you think it'll work this time?" This was her second artificial insemination attempt, after all.

Dr. Grace smiled encouragingly. "Thinking positively doesn't hurt." She patted Emily's arm. "We'll know soon enough. If not, we'll discuss the same options I went over with you before."

"Fertility treatments." Emily didn't relish the possibility, but she'd already foreseen it and had gotten herself an appointment with a famous fertility institute in Massachusetts. But that appointment was nearly six months away and she'd hoped she'd never have to use it.

"Perhaps." The doctor reached for the door. "The nurse will come and let you know when you can get up and get on with the rest of your Friday."

Emily nodded and closed her eyes.

Not only was it artificial insemination Friday, it was "date-night" Friday.

And as she rested there, waiting for the sperm she'd selected out of the hundreds of donor profiles she'd meticulously studied to do its intended job, she couldn't help wondering what else the day would hold for her.

Max had told her to think about "dessert," and in between the back-to-back meetings her assistant had scheduled for her in Atlanta over the past week, she'd thought of little else.

She could hear her cell phone buzzing inside her purse where it was sitting on the side chair just inside the door of the small room. She wasn't supposed to move for a while, but she reached out her arm and managed to snag the handle of her purse and she lifted it onto her belly, quickly pulling out the phone.

It wasn't Max, though.

She sighed, telling herself she had no reason to be disappointed that it wasn't, and pressed a button. "Hey there, Blake," she greeted her little brother. "What's up?"

"Just checking in," he drawled. "Heard you got in from Hot-lanta late last night."

"Yes." She curled her bare toes that felt chilly from the air-conditioning blowing into the room. "I'd have been back earlier if I hadn't had to appease Dad and stand in for *you* with the Connover deal."

"I was meeting with the minister Katie wants to marry us."

It was still hard to believe that the baby boy of the family was getting married. To his assistant, no less. "As much as I admire Katie for taking you on for the long haul, I hope you appreciate my sacrifice."

"What sacrifice? A day and a half less in Red Rock, studying your baby-making spreadsheets?"

She closed her eyes. "It wasn't too long ago you had a thirty-day plan to get a wife," she reminded. It was Blake's business strategy to reunite with his college girlfriend that had inspired her own, equally logical plan to become a mother.

"Yeah, and look how that turned out."

"Just because you came to your senses and realized *Katie* was the one for you and not Finicky Brittany from college doesn't mean your strategy didn't work."

"It was insane to think I could force a relationship into a business plan. Doesn't work any more than putting square blocks in round holes. I just don't want you being disappointed if all of your research and goal-setting doesn't turn out the way you want."

She opened her eyes and stared at the poster

affixed to the ceiling above the examining table. It was a snowy landscape featuring a Cinderella-perfect castle that she happened to know was actually located in Germany. She knew, because she'd visited Neuschwanstein. She was supposed to have been in Frankfurt for a conference, but had snuck out on her own for three days to explore elsewhere.

Her father had been furious. About as furious as he'd been when she'd returned to Red Rock yesterday. He'd been convinced that he'd be able to talk her into staying in Atlanta.

He'd even come close to threatening her with her job.

She wasn't sure anymore if she cared, and for a woman who'd spent her entire life trying to be the model, corporately-aggressive daughter for him, that was quite a question to consider.

"I'm not going to be disappointed," she told her brother now, and very nearly told him what she was doing right that moment, just to prove her point, but discretion won out.

That, and the fact that she rarely shared such private matters with her siblings. Or anyone else for that matter.

Max's face swam in her mind.

"I'm kind of in the middle of something,"

she told Blake. "Unless there's something urgent, I'd better let you go."

"Nothing urgent," he assured. "Tell Wendy hello for me."

Blake and Wendy were nearest to each other in age. They'd always been close. "Will do. And you give Katie a kiss for me."

Blake laughed. "I'll give Katie kisses for *me*," he said, before he rang off.

Emily turned off the phone and dropped it back into her purse. Everyone in the family was finding romance these days. Only she and her eldest brother, Mike, were still single. She wondered if Mike's life were as interesting as hers was at this particular moment...

Remaining where she was, lying on the slightly slanted table, she tossed her purse back onto the chair and rested her head back against the thin, paper-covered pillow once again. "We're finding our own future," she said and patted her abdomen. "Aren't we?"

Then she firmly closed her eyes.

Happy thoughts, she reminded herself.

Again, Max's image swam behind her lids.

Eight more hours, and she'd be with him in person.

Warmth coursed through her at the thought. Decidedly...sensual...warmth.

She opened her eyes and stared at the poster again. It was much less of a turn-on, and considering that she was trying to conceive a baby at that very moment in the most unromantic, scientific of ways, just then felt a whole lot safer.

That evening in San Antonio, Max pointed at the doorway leading off the tree-lined sidewalk. "This is it." A discreet gold sign on the wall next to the door stated Etienne's. He pulled open the door and waited for Emily to enter first.

He couldn't help but absorb the fragrance of her hair as she passed by him. Light. Airy. Every bit as heady as it had been the first time he'd soloed in an airplane. He'd almost been sorry to arrive in San Antonio after the drive from Red Rock, because she'd been sitting beside him in his truck, never knowing that her fragrance had been wrapping around him for the entire drive.

She hesitated inside the dimly lit entrance of the restaurant, waiting for him. Her hair was pulled back as usual, but instead of hanging thick and sleek from the ponytail he was used to seeing, it was twisted into a complicated-looking knot, leaving her neck and shoulders entirely bare except for the narrow straps of the close-fitting ivory dress she wore.

He dragged his eyes from the nape of her neck and met the gaze of the maître d' who was giving Max a tight, superior look. "Reservations?" The guy obviously expected otherwise, and gave a grimace that was probably supposed to pass for a smile when Max gave him his name. "Mr. Allen. I see." His gaze moved to Emily and his smile warmed, probably thinking *she* at least belonged there, before coming back to Max. "If I may speak with you for a moment alone?"

Feeling his nerves tighten, Max followed the tuxedo-clad man a few steps away. "What's wrong?"

"We require our gentlemen to wear jackets and ties, Mr. Allen," the maître d' said.

"You're kidding me."

"We can provide you with a suitable tie," the man went on. "A *loan,*" he added, as if Max were likely to think otherwise.

For a second, Max considered telling the man what he could do with his loaner ties, and leaving. He shoved down the response, though, and considered himself lucky for having at least worn a gray blazer with his button-down white shirt and black jeans. "Thanks."

The maître d' disappeared for a moment and returned with a plain burgundy tie. "The men's room is down the stairs," he said.

Max hid a grimace and returned to Emily, who was looking concerned. "Tie required." He held up the loaner. "I'll be right back."

Before she had a chance to comment, he headed down the short staircase that was to the right of the foyer. He made short work of putting on the tie, then went back up the stairs.

Seemingly satisfied, the maître d' showed them to a small table in a small, sparsely tabled room that was lit only by the heavy iron candle sconces hanging on the walls. "Georges will be your server this evening," he told them, before withdrawing.

Emily smiled across the minuscule table at Max. She was probably used to uptight maître d's. "Considering the lighting in here, nobody but me would even know whether you're wearing a tie or not." Her voice was light.

Max felt heat crawl up his neck, and was acutely glad for that lighting because she probably wouldn't notice. "I should have been more prepared." He could kick himself that he hadn't.

She nudged up her glasses and glanced around at the other tables, only half of which were occupied, then leaned forward a few inches. "I'm taking it that you haven't been here before. So what made you choose it?"

"The food comes highly recommended." But he'd have to tell Brandi she should have warned him about the tie business.

Emily's voice lowered even more. "After the voice mail you left me today, I mentioned to Marcos where we were coming. He told me the chef here is phenomenal." Her smile turned almost mischievous. "And I shouldn't even pass on Wendy's term for his talents."

"What was it?" He wasn't entirely interested in what her sister said, but just then couldn't seem to think of anything beside her skin, which, even in the dimly lit room seemed to glow from some inside source.

Her lashes lowered, almost shyly. "Orgasmic."

His mind felt a lot like a compass needle, suddenly veering north. Emily and orgasms. Not a safe pre-dinner thought, but hardly the first time that combination had crossed his mind. "Seems like a good recommendation," he said before he could think twice.

She laughed softly and sat back, looking up when a skinny, balding man dressed in black from head to toe stopped next to them to introduce himself as Georges. "Your wine selections this evening," he added in his heavy French accent as he handed Max a thick, leather-backed board. "Chef Etienne's recommendations are noted."

Max handed the board to Emily, ignoring the disapproving look that Georges gave him. "You'll know better what you want than me," he told her.

But she didn't even glance at it, just handed the board right back to Georges. Her smile was still in place, but had turned cool. "*Merci,* Georges. *Mais nous n'aurons pas du vin ce soir.*"

"*Très bien, mademoiselle.*" Georges took the board. He switched to English, taking in Max, again. "Shall I bring water, Monsieur?"

"Please."

"Still or sparkling," he prompted, as if Max should have known better than to need prompting.

He wondered what the guy would do if he said *tap.* "Still." He glanced at Emily, who ordered the same.

Georges gave a stiff nod and disappeared.

Max felt like sighing with relief. "What'd you tell him about the wine?"

"Only that we wouldn't be having any."

Max glanced toward the door the waiter had disappeared through. "You didn't have to abstain just because of me."

Warmth returned to her curving lips. "I know." Her fingertips touched the small diamond pendant that dipped just below the enticing hollow at the base of her throat. "I'm actually not a big wine person."

"I'm not sure whether to believe that or not."

She dashed a quick cross over her chest. "Honest."

He kept himself from staring at the invisible cross, positioned tauntingly over the curves beneath the slightly shiny ivory fabric of her dress. "Just margaritas?"

Her fingertip pressed against the diamond, again. "And a really good beer now and then."

"Right." He shook his head. "You don't strike me as the beer type."

She raised her eyebrows. "And what type *do* I strike you as?"

"Champagne and diamonds."

She rolled her eyes. "Is that because I'm a Fortune?"

He stretched his arm across the table and pressed his own fingertip on top of hers, on top of the diamond. "Diamonds," he drawled pointedly.

Her smile seemed to turn a little shaky. She slid her finger from beneath his, but only to press her palm against the thick white tablecloth. "A few diamonds," she allowed softly. "My parents gave me this particular necklace when I turned eighteen."

He lowered his hand next to hers on the table, too. Not touching. But close.

"I'll bet you were—what do they call it? *Finishing school.* I'll bet you were finishing school perfect at eighteen."

She didn't deny it. "And what were you?"

"A hellion. Nobody you'd have wanted to have dinner with at a fast-food dive, much less a place like this. Your parents give you French lessons along the way, too?"

"A few."

"In France?"

Candlelight gleamed over the creamy shoulder she lifted. "A few," she said again. Then she leaned closer once more, her gaze looking at him over the top of her glasses. "I had one tutor who taught me how to swear in three languages."

He laughed outright, earning himself another disapproving look from Georges, who was returning with their water. The waiter set the stemmed glasses in front of them and made a production of pouring the water from a tall, skinny carafe that he left on the table before launching into his accented spiel about their dinner choices.

Max stopped listening after the third choice, which thankfully was the duck that Brandi had mentioned. The other choices were too complicated to even understand.

Emily didn't seem to have any such difficulty, though, and asked a few questions, in French, before making her choice, which seemed to earn Georges's approval before he turned to Max.

"The duck," he said.

Georges waited, eyebrows raised. "It's a prix fixe menu, monsieur. You choose three."

Max wanted to swear. Definitely should have done his research. Maybe then he wouldn't be sitting there while *Georges* snickered behind his disdainful half smile. "I'll have what the lady is having."

"Not…the *duck,* then." Georges's gaze met Max's. He clearly knew that Max was over his head. Max stared back and after a moment, Georges gave that head nod of his again. *"Très bien,"* he said, and backed away.

As soon as the waiter was gone, Emily

leaned forward, her lips pursed in a silent whistle. "He's something, isn't he?"

Max could come up with a few "somethings," but suspected if he uttered the words, the maître d' would call in the cops to have him removed. "Sure you don't want some wine?" At this point, he definitely did. But wanting and having were two different things.

"Absolutely." She shifted and her knee brushed his again. "Did you get any flying in this week?"

He nodded. "A few hours. I'm scheduled to take the exam for my instrument rating next week."

Her smile widened. She immediately picked up her water glass in a toast. "Congratulations!"

He softly clinked his glass against hers. "Thanks. Though congratulations should probably wait until after the test. I might not pass."

"You will."

"Is it a side effect of your job to put a positive spin on everything?"

"Success begins with believing you'll have success." She laughed softly. "That's one of my father's favorite sayings. I guess it's rubbed off over the years. *But,* I can't imagine you not succeeding at something you clearly love."

He could. Easily. For a few short weeks, he'd let himself believe he could be a father. Until reality intruded, proving otherwise.

"What about your week?" Better to get the topic off of him, and back on to her. "Everything go okay in Atlanta?"

Her smile turned to a faint grimace. She set down her glass. "As well as could be expected."

"What does that mean?"

She shook her head, her lashes shielding her gaze. "Nothing interesting, I assure you."

"Everything's interesting when it comes to you," he said bluntly. Truthfully.

Her lashes lifted. She looked surprised. "Well, I had about a hundred meetings—mostly boring—and then—"

"Your Foie Gras Brulee," Georges interrupted, setting two small white plates in front of them with a flourish, along with a dinky basket of triangle toast points.

Max eyed the crusty top of the rounded mound of the pale brown substance in front of him. He didn't know what it was, didn't figure he wanted to know. But he followed Emily's lead, taking one of the small pieces of toast and smearing some of the mound on it.

He gingerly bit off a corner. "Tastes like duck-flavored butter," he said after he'd swallowed.

Emily looked amused. "Don't let Georges hear you. It's most certainly goose, in this place."

"Fine. Tastes like goose butter." He polished off the toast point, and reached for another triangle from the basket. But that one, he ate dry.

Emily was smiling outright now. "Not your taste?"

"I've had worse."

She laughed softly. "So have I." Then she leaned forward and her knee bumped against his again before quickly moving away. "And while this is nicely done, I've also had better." She grinned, a small dimple in her right cheek appearing. "But we won't tell Georges that. Might give him heart palpitations."

"Wouldn't want that." He watched her nibble her way through her own toast points for a moment. Considering everything, she was being a pretty good sport and he felt himself actually begin to relax again. "You wanna give me a heads-up on what else we've got coming?"

"An artichoke soup is next and Cassoulet after that. Cassoulet is pretty much classic French comfort food."

If this restaurant was to be believed, the

French made mounds of butter-smooth fat that tasted like duck. What on earth would they consider comfort food? "I'm afraid to ask what that might be."

She nudged aside the appetizer plate and touched the corners of her lips daintily with her big, linen napkin. "Good old bean and meat casserole," she drawled. "Meat varies. Pork. Chicken. Could be nearly anything. Even duck."

"The other parts of that goose?"

She sat forward a little. "Don't know. Possibly. Shall we call out Georges and ask him?"

Max shook his head. "Pass."

She chuckled.

He had to shift less than two inches and his knee found hers. He let it stay there.

So did she.

He decided that choking down some unusual dishes wouldn't be the worst thing he'd ever done. Not as long as he had Emily there for company.

Before long, Georges returned, replacing their plates with shallow bowls of a creamy, pale soup.

That, at least, came close to living up to Emily's brother-in-law's assessment. It was delicious, and Max finished every drop.

But that, too, seemed to be gauche, if Georges's faint sneer as he collected Max's empty bowl and Emily's half-empty bowl was any estimation.

While they'd been there, the other tables had slowly become occupied. Women wearing diamonds and black dresses—most considerably skimpier than Emily's dress—and men wearing suits and ties.

Emily, who was lovelier than any of the women, fit in among them like a glove.

Max, though, in his black jeans and gray sports coat and *loaner* red tie, felt as though he stuck out like a sore thumb.

The only comfort—and distraction—was that Emily still hadn't moved her leg and the spot where their knees touched just kept getting warmer. And warmer.

"Compliments of Chef Etienne." The maître d' seemed to appear out of nowhere. He was cradling a bottle of wine as if it were the greatest gift. "Had we realized earlier we were being treated to your company, Ms. Fortune, he would have delighted in presenting you with a special menu, as well."

Max stared. Emily looked equally surprised. But she recovered a lot faster. "That's very kind of Chef Etienne," she replied. "But truly not necessary. I don't even—"

"For Chef, it's very necessary," the maître d' insisted, busily uncorking the bottle, and handing the cork to Max. He gestured to a young man nearby, who quickly set two wineglasses on the table.

"Thank you," Emily said again. "Please tell the chef thank you for us." She touched the bottle that the maître d' was preparing to pour over Max's glass. "However, we'll pour if you don't mind?"

The maître d' looked pained. But he set the bottle on the table. *"Certainement."* Then he walked stiffly away.

Max heard Emily sigh. "I'm sorry," she said. "I don't know how they even know who I am."

"Nothing to be sorry for," he assured. He lifted the bottle to pour some into her glass, but she stretched her hand out at the same time and he missed her glass altogether. He muttered an oath, righting the bottle quickly, but still managing to send a good amount of the rich, dark wine right over her hand and the blindingly white tablecloth.

She quickly swiped her napkin over her hand and dropped it over the mess, but not quickly enough to keep the wine from dripping off the table onto her lap.

Max's nerves tightened all over again. Dark wine. Ivory dress. This was worse than the damned loaner tie.

He should have stuck to Red. It was about as fancy as he could manage without making an ass out of himself.

Better yet, he should have realized it was pointless trying to impress Emily.

"I'm sorry," he muttered, slapping his own napkin over the spreading wine.

"It's not your fault," she assured quickly. But as she started to stand, he saw just how much wine had hit her dress.

He knew enough about women to know there was no way to redeem the evening.

Georges had returned, too, giving Max a sidelong glare as he swiftly removed the tablecloth. The same kid who'd brought the wineglasses was there, too, with replacement linens.

"I'll take you home," Max said to Emily. He slid his wallet out of his pocket, pulled out his credit card and handed it to Georges, hoping like hell the man would have some sense and keep his mouth shut. He could feel nearly every eye in the place on them. Georges palmed the card and scurried away.

"That's not necessary," Emily protested. She felt the promise of the evening spinning further out of her grasp, but sat down again anyway, unfolding her fresh napkin over her lap. "Max, it's *fine*." She was well aware that he didn't feel comfortable at the restaurant, and would have done nearly anything to make him feel more at ease.

He remained standing, though. "It's not fine." He turned toward Georges when the waiter reappeared and scribbled his name inside the small leather folder.

Emily could only imagine the amount of the check and even though she could have easily offered to pay, she wouldn't have dreamed of treading on Max's toes that way.

Then Georges turned toward her, giving her the generous smile that he'd stingily withheld from Max all evening. "Mademoiselle Fortune," he gushed. "Perhaps you would consider being Chef's guest another night? It would be our pleasure to see you again."

Her. Not Max.

She smiled back at him as she stood. Not caring in the least about the wine splattered over her lap, she stepped around to Max's side and deliberately began loosening the knot of his tie, boldly ignoring the start he gave. "If Mr. Allen considers returning, then perhaps I will," she told Georges.

Then she smiled up into Max's face as she slowly slid the tie out from beneath his collar. She even flicked open the top two buttons of his white shirt to reveal the strong, bronzed column of his throat.

Aware that they had more of an audience than the irritating Georges, she squashed the intriguing interest in undoing several more buttons and instead draped the tie carelessly over the back of his chair. "Now," she said to Max, "why don't we go somewhere we'll actually *enjoy?*"

Chapter 6

"I wasn't joking in there," Emily said once they were outside the restaurant.

Max looked at her. His expression was grim. "I appreciate the cheerleading act in there, but you don't have to keep it up." He yanked his blazer off his shoulders and closed his fist around it. "I'll pay to have your dress cleaned. And if it doesn't come clean, I'll pay to replace it."

She managed not to sigh. The dress was one-of-a-kind, designed by a friend of hers, which she had no intention of admitting. "Max, I don't *care* about the dress." She sent silent apologies to Lydia, but it was the absolute truth.

"I do." He headed along the sidewalk. It was illuminated by an occasional street lamp, but otherwise, the tree-lined walkway was dark.

She took a few skipping steps to catch up to him. "Max, please slow down. I can't keep up."

He immediately stopped. "Sorry."

She slowed, too, and stopped in front of him. "I was really looking forward to this evening."

"And I ruined it."

"No!" She pushed her fingers through her hair, only to remember too late that Wendy had helped pin it up. She shoved the loosened pins back into place. "That's not what I am saying at all."

He gave her a disbelieving look. "You *like* going places to have wine dumped on you?"

"Spilling that wine was just as much my fault as it was yours. I didn't even want it!" She wouldn't be drinking any sort of alcohol as long as the possibility remained that her appointment earlier that day was successful. "I still don't know how the chef even realized I was your date. If anyone ruined the evening, it was me."

"I doubt you've ever ruined anything in your life, and tonight wasn't the start." He threw his head back, looking up at the canopy of trees over their heads.

She wondered if he was trying to see the sky. Imagining himself far from earth, from her, in an airplane up there. "I don't exist in a vacuum of perfection," she told him. "I'm just like everyone else." She dashed her hands over her stained dress. "Unexpected things happen all the time." Meeting him, for one.

He finally looked back at her. He didn't look happy, but at least that terribly grim expression had eased. "I wanted to impress you."

Her knees went a little weak. "With a fancy French restaurant?"

"I figured it was a little early in the game for diamonds."

Definitely weak. But she took it as a good sign that his tone had turned a little wry. "I'm actually happier with more casual things. Simple pleasures. You know. Like—" She broke off, feeling unusually tentative. She moistened her lips. "Like fiery food at places like Red. Sunday afternoon picnics. Friday nights spent in. Just tossing a few steaks on the grill." She hadn't actually done some of those things, but that didn't mean they didn't sound perfect to her.

He still didn't look convinced.

"I put a lot more importance on *who* I'm spending time with, than where we're doing it."

His eyebrow peaked ever so slightly and she felt her cheeks warm a little when she realized how her words could be misconstrued. "I mean where we're *spending time*."

"Mmm." The corners of his lips actually curved a little. "Not sure that sounds as interesting."

She pressed her lips together for a moment, confining her own smile. She wasn't sure it sounded as interesting, either, but only because it was Max she was thinking about. She'd never met another man who had the ability to make her want to forget everything except him.

"It's still early," she said. "We don't have to call an end to things just because of those people in there." She jerked her head over her shoulder in the direction of the restaurant.

"Where am I going to take you with your dress dripping with wine?"

It was hardly dripping. It was damp, yes. And the red wine would probably never come out of the ivory summer-weight wool. "What about your place?" Her heart thumped hard against the scooped bodice. Not once in her entire life had she so openly thrown herself at a man.

She'd already noticed that he was an uncommonly still man. He didn't fidget. Rarely appeared restless. But with her suggestion seeming to hang in the heated evening air, he seemed to grow even more still.

"I live in an apartment."

She swallowed past the knot in her throat. "Alone?"

"You know the answer to that."

Yes. She did. He lived alone, and she knew it because he'd told her so, himself. "I'm staying with my sister." Something he knew, equally well.

He watched her for what seemed like an eternity. She could feel perspiration popping out on the back of her neck. The small of her back. Wasn't certain if it was owed to the summer evening, or to him.

"I have soda and a few steaks in the fridge." He smiled slightly. "Maybe some ice cream in the freezer. It's probably not particularly sinful or rich but it *is* chocolate."

Tension oozed out of her only to be replaced by an intoxicating liquid heat. "Works for me." She sounded breathless and didn't care one little bit. She didn't know what exactly she was inviting, didn't know what he thought she was inviting, but that wasn't something she cared about, either.

She was with Max.

And right then, that was all that mattered.

They made the drive back to Red Rock in silence. Max lived in an upstairs apartment, and Emily nearly swallowed her tongue when he pressed his hand against the small of her back, guiding her up the steps. At the top, he unlocked the door and reached inside to flip a light switch before nudging her inside and closing the door.

"I'll get you something to change into if you want to get out of that dress."

She didn't trust herself to answer that so she just nodded and he headed out of the living area and disappeared down the hallway.

Alone, she let her curiosity take hold. The apartment was pretty standard, with tan carpet and ivory walls. He had an L-shaped brown couch behind which stood the floor lamp that he'd turned on at the wall switch, an oversize beige recliner and an enormous flat-screen television filling up the space of the living room. On the other side of the doorway was a small dining area complete with a simple round table and four chairs, and a kitchen with a breakfast bar. Two bar stools were tucked beneath the bar.

What really held her interest, though, was the brick fireplace in the corner opposite the couch and she aimed straight for it, dropping her purse on the couch along the way. Three framed photographs were on the plain black shelf that served as a mantel.

The first was a family shot that looked to be several years old, with a young Max standing between his sister who was wearing a graduation cap and gown and an older woman. Judging by the resemblance, it was probably their mother. The second was much more recent of just Max and Kirsten—this time wearing a wedding gown. And the third was a close-up shot of a fat-cheeked baby.

Her heart squeezed as she slowly picked up the small frame to take a closer look. Was this little Anthony? The baby he'd given up?

"They'll be too big, but at least I can promise they're clean." Max's voice preceded him back into the room and Emily quickly stuck the picture frame back on the mantel.

But not quickly enough, she realized as she turned toward him.

His gaze immediately cut to the picture, but

all he did was extend a bundle of faded gray toward her. "The shorts have a drawstring so you can tighten 'em up. Bathroom's down the hall."

Emily took the bundle from him and almost asked about the baby in the picture. But he was already sliding open the arcadia door next to the television and she saw the outline of a covered gas grill on the small outdoor terrace.

Clutching the clothing, she quickly found the bathroom and closed herself inside. There was nothing fancy about the finishes there, but everything looked scrupulously clean and the light bar was unrelentingly bright. It clearly showed off her flushed cheeks in the mirror behind the sink vanity.

Looking away from herself and the dress—which looked worse than she'd expected it to—she pulled down the side zipper hidden beneath her arm and let it fall to the floor. She kicked off her pumps and stepped out of the dress, then reached for the clothes he'd left her.

Only when she slid the washed-soft T-shirt over her head did she think about the fact that all she'd worn beneath the dress had been a thin pair of lace panties. The lined dress possessed a built-in bra and Emily had eschewed wearing nylons because of the warm weather.

She inhaled slowly and looked at herself in the mirror, chewing the inside of her cheek. Not even the fading Texas Rangers logo on the front of the cotton knit shirt could disguise the clearly visible points of her nipples that had drawn up tight the second she'd pulled on *his* shirt.

The only saving grace was that the shirt was so large on her, she was practically swimming in it.

She pressed her hands over her breasts, imagining Max's hands doing the same.

Then she shook her head sharply and dropped her hands.

What was wrong with her?

Yes, she was attracted to Max. But she felt like she was about ready to melt from the inside out and she could feel her pulse pounding dizzily through every inch of her body. Head to toe and all points in between. She'd never felt so ridiculously out of control before.

She quickly turned on the faucet and ran cold water over her wrists. Then she grabbed the gray gym shorts and pulled them on, fiddling with the drawstring inside the waistband until it was tight enough not to slide down past her hips. The loose-fitting shorts probably reached Max's knees, but on her, they extended well below.

There was nothing remotely sexy about the too-large getup. And she wasn't sure she'd ever felt more aroused than she did just from wearing clothes that he'd obviously worn.

She quickly gathered up her dress, going through the motions of soaking the stained portion in the sink even though she doubted it could be saved, before leaving the bathroom.

As soon as she reached the living room, she could smell the steaks, already on the grill. But a noise from the kitchen had her turning that direction.

Max had changed, too, exchanging his button-down for a white Redmond Flight School T-shirt that had the sleeves ripped out. She carefully kept her eyes from staring too long at the roping muscles revealed by the shirt as she slid onto one of the bar stools. "This is a nice place you have."

"It's a place to sleep." He barely glanced at her as he slid a tall glass of ice onto the bar in front of her. "I've got tea and water, too, if you don't want soda."

"Water works." Dr. Grace had lectured her more than once how important it was that she drank more water.

He pulled out a bottle of filtered water from the fridge and filled her glass and with a minimum of motion, rotated to put the large bottle back in the fridge.

She blindly wrapped her hand around the glass, staring at his backside. All too quickly, he was facing her again, and she could feel her cheeks getting warm all over again. She sipped at the water with one hand and below the breakfast bar surreptitiously plucked the front of the shirt away from her aching breasts. "How, um, how long have you lived here?"

"Little less than a year." He pulled the tab on a can of cola and took a long drink. "I was living with my sister before that. And you? What do you call home?"

Watching him swallow that long drink was better than any commercial she'd ever seen. He could have been selling deep-fried worms and she'd want to stock up.

She moistened her lips, feeling parched despite the water. "Red Rock feels like home lately," she replied faintly.

His lips tilted. "You like the live-in babysitter role that much?"

She shifted on the padded seat. Everywhere the clothes hit, her skin felt hot. Strangely, sensually tight. "Actually, I love babysitting

MaryAnne. I never get tired of it." A thin vein of remaining common sense had her shying away from the topic of babies. Any baby. "But Wendy and Marcos are still newlyweds and their house is barely big enough for them."

"Cramping their style a little?"

She nodded, lifting the glass to her lips again and drinking thirstily as she looked toward his living room. "I've begun investigating finding a place of my own," she said when she set the glass down again. "Do you know if there are any units available here?"

He leaned down over the breakfast bar on his bent arms, his hands only inches from the one she had clenched around the sweating water glass. "This place would be slumming for you, wouldn't it?"

She nudged up her glasses and angled her chin, giving him a look. "I live in a two-bedroom, one-bath apartment back in Atlanta."

"Which you probably own."

She couldn't deny that. The loft-style condo had been a very good investment. "If you have such a problem with my family's money, why did you even ask me out tonight?"

"I told you I found you interesting."

"The front page of the newspaper is interesting."

"And because I can't look at you without wanting you."

Parched hadn't even begun to describe things. Her lips parted, but her suddenly addled brain couldn't begin to frame a response.

"But that's just about sex," he added after a moment.

"Ah," she said faintly. "Sex."

"And the hitch isn't just your money," he went on, sounding dogged.

"My family's money," she corrected. She earned a very nice salary but she still supported her own expenses.

"You're also my boss's sister-in-law," he finished as if she hadn't spoken at all. "So, like it or not, sleeping with you isn't...smart."

"Put that way, I suppose it probably isn't." She picked up the glass and took a gulp. When she set the glass down, her knuckles bumped his fingers.

And she froze when he slid those blunt-tipped, warm fingers over the back of her hand, then slipped to the inside of her wrist, pressing right against her rocketing pulse.

"Problem is—" His voice dropped a notch. His fingers slowly inched upward from her inner wrist until they reached the crook of her elbow. "I usually make a habit of doing things that aren't smart."

"Like what?"

He just shook his head, though. His gaze was locked on hers.

There were only inches separating her arm from the side of her breast. If she moved at all, his fingertips would brush against her. She inhaled slowly, unconsciously deep. "Max."

"I really can't afford not being smart anymore, Emily."

Common sense warred with desire. She'd been the one to suggest coming back to his place. "Do you want me to leave?" She didn't wait for an answer, but quickly slipped off the bar stool. "Never mind." Maybe he felt like he couldn't honestly answer, considering everything. "I never meant to put you in an awkward position, Max."

He gave a low, choking sort of laugh. "Too late."

She could feel heat creeping into her face again. "I'll just, um, get my dress. I left it soaking in the sink." She headed around the breakfast bar for the hallway.

But he moved quickly, his arm catching her around the waist, hauling her up against him.

"If I hadn't wanted you to come back here, you wouldn't be here."

Her hips were squared off against him and there was no mistaking his arousal. She pressed her palms flat against his chest, staring fiercely at his jaw while she struggled with her own. It would be so, so easy to give in. But at what cost?

He'd end up considering it a mistake. Another one of his not-smart moves.

And she'd be left with his regret.

"We just take it out of the equation," she said abruptly.

"What?" His fingers flexed against her waist. Slid around to the small of her back.

She ruthlessly cut off the wish that his hands would slip even lower. Grip her even tighter against him. "Sex." Her throat felt tight and she had to force out the word. "We take sex off the table."

His head lowered. His mouth brushed against her temple. Burned against her cheek. "I think sex on the table sounds pretty sweet." His whisper was rough and hot near her ear.

Her knees turned to gelatin, her overactive mind conjuring the feel of him laying her back against that round table, shoving the chairs out of their way—

She grasped for her rapidly dissolving common sense. "And we could just—" she broke off, inhaling sharply when she felt his teeth close over her earlobe, tugging slightly "—just...*ah*...just be friends."

He shifted slightly, his leg nudging between hers as his hand slid beneath the loose T-shirt. Grazed up her bare spine and dragged slowly down again, sliding right over the curve of her rear and pulling her in even more tightly. "Right," he drawled. "That's gonna happen." He kissed the point of her chin. The corner of her mouth.

She pulled her head back, staring up at him. "You just said this wasn't smart."

His eyes looked nearly black. "And I also said I was good at doing what wasn't smart. Welcome to my world." He slid his hand along her jaw. "Take off your glasses." His fingertips found the nape of her neck and his thumb brushed over the corner of her mouth. His thumb pressed gently, slipping between her lips.

If it hadn't been for his hard thigh notched between hers and the arm he still had around her, Emily's legs would have simply given way. She mindlessly pulled off her glasses, tossing them carelessly on the breakfast bar while the tip of her tongue pressed against his thumb. Tasting salt. Tasting him.

She felt the breath he sucked in, and then his fingers dug into her nape, tilting her head back even more and his mouth covered hers.

His lips were surprisingly soft. His taste sweet. Like his soda. Only so much more appetizing.

Then he made a sound low in his throat and lifted his head only long enough for them both to catch their breaths before kissing her again. Deeper. Harder.

Her hands slid out from between them, going behind his neck. Sliding up into his thick, tantalizingly silky hair. Her breasts felt crushed against his hard chest and she reveled in it. And then his hands were moving again, finding her hips, rocking her against him; sliding down, underneath the waistband that she'd tightened with the string; down, beneath the lace of her panties, his fingertips burning against her bare derriere as he urged her forward, forward.

She dragged her mouth from his, pressing her head into the curve of his shoulder, gasping his name as everything inside her seemed to tighten, spiraling higher and higher. "Max. Please. You're going to make me—" She broke off, hardly believing what she was doing, much less what she was saying.

"Good." In a swift motion, he yanked her T-shirt over her head. She heard the faint ping of hairpins as they came loose and her hair unraveled. "I want to make you come." He clearly had no such verbal reservations. "Again." He caught one breast in his hand, his fingers taunting her exquisitely rigid nipple. "And again." His lips found the other.

Her fingers jerkily tangled in his hair, her head falling forward. She couldn't help the sobbing moan that rose inside her when his other hand slid between them, arrowing straight between her thighs.

It took a while for the sound of chimes to penetrate. At first, she thought it was only inside her head. The twenty-first-century version of hearing violins as she hovered on the brink of the orgasm he was driving her straight toward.

But then Max lifted his head. He sucked in a deep breath. "Damn it." His hand left her aching breast. Slipped even more slowly away from the moist lace.

The chimes repeated. Insistently.

He set her aside, yanked his shirt over his jeans and stepped around her.

He was heading for the front door.

Only then did she realize the chiming had been the doorbell. She snatched up the Rangers T-shirt and clutched it against her bare breasts, turning to lean back against the short kitchen wall where she'd be out of sight of the front door.

She sucked in a shaking breath and fumbled with her eyeglasses, putting them back in place.

"Hello, Mrs. Sheckley," she heard him say in greeting. "What's up?"

"Max, dearie. I wanted to see if you were all right."

"Perfect, Mrs. Sheckley. Why?"

"Well, honey, something's burning on your grill."

Emily pressed her face into the T-shirt. Of course. The steaks. She soundlessly pulled on the shirt and peered cautiously around the corner of the wall. Mrs. Sheckley looked about five feet tall and ninety years old and she was looking up at Max as if he were her favorite person in the world.

Max glanced over his shoulder, catching Emily peeking. He gave her a wry grimace before turning back to his visitor. "Thanks,

Mrs. Sheckley. Guess I got distracted. I'll pull 'em off."

Mrs. Sheckley patted his cheek, then pushed a plastic-wrapped plate into his hands. "I brought you some of those cookies you like," she said. "But you be sure to eat something else, too, now," she instructed before she disappeared from Emily's view.

Emily stepped out of the kitchen once Max closed the door.

"Sorry about that," he told her.

"Maybe you should be saying 'saved by the bell.'" She still felt like an inferno was burning her up from the inside out, but the interruption had at least allowed her common sense to rear its head once more. "I don't want anything to happen that you're going to regret."

He shoved his fingers through his hair as he crossed the room to the terrace, dumping the plate that Mrs. Sheckley had left him on the coffee table in front of the couch along the way. Outside, he transferred the steaks from the grill to a plate but left them sitting on the small table next to the grill. "What I regret is answering the damn door," he said when he came back in.

Emily smiled slightly. She shook her head. "You don't mean that."

He gave her a long look. "Steaks weren't the only thing burning. I'm still hard and I know exactly how I want you to help me deal with that."

An ache twisted through her. Her legs actually shook. "None of the reasons why you said this wasn't smart have disappeared in the last few minutes."

"Hey." His lips twisted wryly. "Give a guy some credit. *Twenty* minutes."

She felt a smile touch her own lips. "I kind of felt like time was standing still, actually."

His eyes darkened. He took a step toward her.

Her pulse seemed to stutter, then bolted past the starting gate all over again.

She knew if he touched her, she'd lose that moment's grace of common sense. Was afraid that his touch might not even be necessary for her to lose it. "I should go."

"Is that what you really want?"

"No." She lifted her shoulders, feeling torn. It wasn't a sensation she was particularly familiar with. "But it's probably *smart*."

He exhaled noisily. "Fine. I'll take you home." Then he picked up the plate that Mrs. Sheckley had left and his lips tilted crookedly. "But first you've got to help me eat these things. She's a sweet lady. I bring in her paper for her every morning and she returns the favor by baking for me. But she can't bake worth squat. Everything comes out burnt." He peeled off the plastic wrap and plucked a dark-edged cookie off the pile to take a bite. "Oatmeal-raisin. I think."

She studied him for a moment. "You *could* just throw them away, you know."

"Could. But it'd hurt her feelings if she knew." He extended the plate toward her.

He'd eat burnt cookies just to save his neighbor's feelings.

She smiled, and slowly reached out for one of the cookies. But she was shaking inside.

Fireworks she could handle.

This strange ache inside her heart, though?

That was another matter entirely.

Chapter 7

"Turn sharper," Max said urgently. "You're going to run off the cliff again."

Emily jerked the wheel in her hand, her attention glued to the action on Max's big television. Her character—an ape named Priscilla—went spiraling off the edge of the animated mountain, landing with a splash in the rippling water at the base.

Emily tossed the gaming wheel onto the couch between her and Max and leaned back. "I'm done. *Finis.* I'll never get the hang of this stupid game."

Max tsked. "Is that negativity I hear actually coming from your lips?"

Emily grimaced but there wasn't a lot of heat in it.

Once she and Max had polished off Mrs. Sheckley's half-dozen cookies—helped copiously by the glasses of milk that Max had poured—he *should* have driven Emily home. Instead, they'd somehow found themselves sitting side by side on the couch, pitting their skills against a computer video game and each other.

She still wasn't quite sure how that had come about.

And now, well past midnight, there was an opened box of half-eaten pizza sitting on the coffee table in front of them. "I've killed off poor Priscilla five times on that curve," she told Max. He was steering his own character—an unlikely androgynous dragonlike beast named Julio—to the finish line of the race. "It's time I stopped torturing poor Priscilla, don't you think? It's not negativity if it's just plain fact."

"Sounds like advertising spin, if you ask me."

For the past few hours, she'd miraculously managed to concentrate on something *other* than the fact that his bedroom was merely steps away, but as he tossed aside his own game wheel and stretched, she quickly realized how tenuous that control was. "I should get home."

His gaze cut to her. "Or...you could stay."

Her mouth went as dry as the Sahara. How easy it would be to nod. To just go with the moment.

He'd take her to bed.

They'd make love.

There'd be fireworks going off all over the place.

And then morning would come. Always, morning would come.

He'd decide it had all been a mistake and move on, and she'd be left as alone as ever. Only with the added knowledge of what being with him—even for that short while—could be like. Sometimes ignorance was the smarter choice. She couldn't miss what she didn't know.

"I *could* stay." Her voice was husky.

His gaze was steady. "But you won't," he finished.

She wordlessly shook her head.

He exhaled. "This is a hell of a note, isn't it?"

Wordless still, she nodded.

And after a moment, he did, too. "Okay."

He pushed to his feet. "Get your things and I'll grab the keys."

She rose, also, and hurried into the bathroom. Her dress had been soaking in the sink for the past few hours. The wine stains hadn't gone anywhere and there was no way she could wear the garment. She squeezed out the water and rolled it into a ball, then tucked her high-heeled pumps on top and returned to the living room.

Max was waiting by the opened door, staring at the keys he was jingling from his finger and wondering what the hell he was doing when Emily reappeared.

She added her small clutch handbag to the pile in her arms and stepped out onto the landing. "I'll get your clothes back to you as soon as I can."

He pulled the door shut. "No hurry." His fingers touched the small of her back and she quickened her step, hurrying down the staircase that his apartment shared with his neighbor as if she didn't want him touching her.

Considering the way she'd practically gone up in flames when he had, though, he had a hard time believing it.

They reached the sidewalk and she stopped to slip her feet into her shoes. "I probably look like a 'Fashion Don't' picture out of a magazine."

"It's definitely a different look for you." Max held her arm as they crossed the parking lot to the covered spot. "I think I like it," he admitted.

Her soft laughter rang out in the still night. "Oversize men's workout togs and four-inch heels. You're just being polite."

"I'm being polite *not* telling you what goes through a man's mind when the woman he wants is wearing nothing much more *than* his shirt and a pair of sexy high heels." He liked looking at her on an ordinary day with her hair smooth and neat as a pin, her slender body wrapped in one of her stylishly tailored suits. Seeing her this way—wholly untailored with her hair tumbling messily around her shoulders, soft lips bare and ridiculously inviting— was damn near painful.

It was too easy to forget she was supposed to be out of his league.

They'd reached his truck and he pulled open the passenger door for her. She was hugging the bundle of her clothing to her stomach. Her lips were rounded in a silent "Oh."

"If you don't get in now, I'm going to try real hard to convince you to stay," he warned.

She moistened her lips and hesitated for a moment just long enough to have him nearly groaning out loud. But then she ducked her chin and climbed up onto the high seat.

His fingers clenched the door hard for a second before he shut it quietly and went around to the driver's side.

The streets were empty at that time of night and it seemed to take only minutes to drive from his apartment on one side of Red Rock to her sister's place on the other.

"Don't get out," she told him when he pulled up at the curb. The porch light clearly illuminated the front door and most of the walkway leading up to it. "I really did enjoy myself, Max. Even Mrs. Sheckley's cookies."

"You still need that flying lesson," he said abruptly.

She gave him a quick look, her brows pulling together. "Why? You're doing fine with everything on your own."

"Tanner's on board with the website changes," he reminded. "And he agrees about the social media angle for the high schools. I don't know anything about that stuff. It was your idea in the first place."

She hesitated. Looked as if she wanted to say something. But after a moment, she nodded. "True enough. So, schedule the lesson then, and let me know when you want me to meet you at the office again."

He was damn glad for the chance Tanner was giving him, but right then he couldn't have cared less about the office.

It was an excuse to see her again, plain and simple. A safe excuse.

"I'll talk to Ross and let you know when."

She nodded and slid out of the truck, but hesitated before closing the door as she looked back at him. "If it makes any difference, I'd rather just go flying with you." Her voice was soft. Not exactly hesitant, but not exactly confident, either.

The gnawing ache in his gut reached new proportions. "How 'bout Sunday?"

Her eyes widened a little. "Okay."

"Okay." He'd have to juggle a few things to make sure a plane was available. "We'll need to be at the airport in the afternoon."

She was giving him that soft half smile of hers. She nodded. "I'll meet you there." She finally shut the door and headed up the walkway toward the house. On the porch, she looked back and gave a brief wave before disappearing inside.

Only then did Max exhale and drive away.

It was past midnight. But it wasn't his bed he wanted to get to.

It was a cold, *cold* shower.

"So?" Kirsten eyed him over the plate of cinnamon rolls she was holding. "How'd it go?"

It was Sunday morning and he was at Kirsten's place for breakfast. Ostensibly to eat the food that Jeremy wouldn't be, because he was at the hospital. Max figured his sister was more concerned with pumping him for information than she was with any food going to waste. But this way he didn't have to cook for himself, so he figured he could tolerate it.

He was in a good mood, anyway.

It was Sunday.

He'd be flying that afternoon.

With Emily.

He transferred two rolls off the tray to his plate. "How'd what go?"

"Don't play dumb. You took Emily over to San Antonio for dinner, didn't you?"

He chewed his way through half of a roll before nodding. "Yeah."

Kirsten's eyebrows climbed halfway up her forehead. "And…?"

He shrugged. "And nothing." He sure as hell

wasn't going to tell his sister about what had gone on—or not gone on—when he and Emily had returned to his place.

Her lips compressed. She plopped down on her seat across the breakfast table from him. "Talkative as always," she complained. She poured herself a mug of coffee. "What restaurant did you go to?"

His good humor hit a small pothole. "Place called Etienne's. One of the instructors out at Redmond recommended it."

Kirsten was nodding. "Jeremy's taken me there."

Figured. Max doubted the surgeon had made the mistake of going without his own necktie. He pulled off another corner of the roll and shoved it in his mouth.

"Food was wonderful," his sister was saying. "But Jeremy thought the atmosphere was a little stuffy." She nudged a bowl of scrambled eggs toward him. "Have some eggs. You need protein, too."

"Sure thing, Mother." But he scooped some eggs on his plate anyway. Mostly because he wanted them.

"Ha-ha. So what'd you have to eat?"

He eyed her. "You really want to know what was on the menu?"

"Nooo." She pinched off a piece of roll and nibbled at it. "But I figure at least that's something you'll be willing to talk about."

He sighed. No matter what ups and downs the two of them had experienced together, he did know that she had his best interests at heart. "Goose butter," he finally said, a little wryly. "Some seriously nasty stuff in my opinion but Emily seemed to like it okay."

His sister started to smile. "Jeremy doesn't like it much, either."

"Knew there was something I liked about him."

"So what else?"

"Soup. We never got to the entrée. And don't start looking all excited. I spilled wine all over her and we left."

Her expression fell. "Was she angry?"

Far from it. "Didn't seem to be. How well does your husband know that side of the family?"

"The Atlanta Fortunes. That's what he calls them, anyway." She sipped her coffee. "And I asked him that myself after we ran into you two at Red. He said they'd never been particularly close." She didn't look concerned. "Jeremy and his brothers grew up in California. William was busy running Fortune Forecasting there. It wasn't connected to Fortune-South at all, except for the name. I think it was mostly a cards-at-Christmas sort of relationship. He did say that John Michael—Emily's father?—is pretty hard-driving. Everyone in the family evidently thinks so."

What Max knew about FortuneSouth was what he'd looked up on the internet the day after he'd met Emily in Tanner's office. He'd found a slick website for the telecommunications company that covered more things than he'd been interested in clicking through and then a boatload of independent news articles that he'd read a lot more closely.

Enough to confirm what he'd already suspected. Emily was way out of his league. He hadn't discovered anything in the few weeks since then to change his mind.

"I'm still a little stunned that you and Emily are dating when I hadn't even known you'd met."

"We're not dating."

Kirsten's eyebrows shot up again. "What do you call it then?"

"Hell if I know," he muttered. "They have a lot of money."

Kirsten was silent for a moment. "And that bothers you. Obviously."

He polished off the eggs and moved on to his second roll.

"Max, if you like her, then all that shouldn't matter."

"It matters."

"Why? I come from the same background as you and *I* married a Fortune."

"You're a woman. It's different if the guy's the one with no dough."

She made a face. "Talk about double standards."

He shrugged. "Maybe. But still true." He didn't look at his sister. "What do I have to offer a woman like her?"

"A lot." She reached across the table, squeezing his arm. "You're kind and caring and loyal."

He grunted, scooting back from the table. "Like a damn lapdog."

"You're also ridiculously stubborn, judge people too quickly, are way too hard on yourself and refuse to let yourself believe that good things can happen to you and they can last."

He carried his plate to the sink. "In my experience, things *don't* last," he reminded. "And I was a screwup." He gave her a look when she started to protest. "We both know it," he cut her off.

"You just took a while to find your footing. You know, Max." She hesitated for a moment. "I'm really proud of you. After you gave up Anthony—"

He stiffened, gave her a warning look that, as usual, she ignored.

"Well, I wasn't sure how you'd handle all of that," she said. "But look at you. You got into flying and now you work at the flight school. You have a nice place of your own. Everything's coming together."

"Spoken like a loyal sister. Until I screw everything up again."

She shook her head. "You're not going to do anything of the sort. That's not the man you've become. I just wish you'd lighten up where Anthony is concerned."

"I just wish you'd quit while you were ahead." He left the plate in the sink and kissed the top of her head. "Thanks for the grub. Tell your husband I appreciate eating his share."

"Max." She trailed after him as he headed for the front door.

He shook his head. "No, Kirsten. Not this time. I know you still see him." He couldn't even say Anthony's name. "That's fine." Jeremy and Coop were cousins and Kirsten had fallen in love with that baby boy same as Max had. "But he's got a father now. Last thing he needs is me being around, confusing him. Topic closed."

Her disagreement showed plainly, but he appreciated the fact that she didn't voice any more of it. She just waved when he left.

After Kirsten's, he visited the deli department at the supermarket and ordered a few sandwiches. He'd borrowed a basket the day before from Mrs. Sheckley. She'd been nearly beside herself at the notion that he had a date and had added a bag of brownies that more closely resembled hockey pucks and talked for an hour about the picnics that she and her husband had taken when they'd been young.

He added several bottles of lemonade and water to the sandwiches, and an enormous chocolate bar that was sure to be more edible than the brownies and eyed the bunches of cut flowers stuck in a bucket of water next to the checkout register. There was no point in pretending he'd ever be the kind of man who'd give Emily hothouse roses.

He ignored the flower bunches and put his purchases in front of the young clerk.

"Looks like lunch," the girl said, giving him a flirtatious smile. "I've seen you here before. Max, right?"

He nodded and wished he'd gone to the other checkout even though the other clerk had a line twice as long.

"I'm Tammy," she said, even though he hadn't asked and could see the tag on her uniform perfectly well. She slowly moved the lemonades over the conveyor belt. "Are you sharing these with someone special?"

Two years before, maybe even as recently as a year ago, he'd have been perfectly willing to take advantage of the opening she was throwing at him. She was young. Cute.

His speed.

He grabbed a bunch of daisies out of the bucket and added it to his items before pulling out his wallet. "Yeah."

She gave a smile that seemed to say "Oh, well," wished him a nice day and in minutes, he was out the door only to come face-to-face with Cooper Fortune.

Max's nerves knotted as he immediately looked around, but he saw no sign of Cooper's wife, Kelsey, or his son. And before Max could avoid it, Cooper had stuck out his hand in greeting. "Max. How's everything?"

"Good. You?" Max shook the other man's hand, keeping it as brief as possible, sidestepping along the way. It wasn't that he didn't like

Cooper Fortune. He didn't know him all that well. Except to know the man pretty much had everything that Max had once wanted.

Namely, Anthony.

"Everything's great," Cooper said.

"Good to hear." Max managed a smile and sidestepped again, holding up the bulging bag in his hand. The daisies were poking out the top of it. "Gotta book." He didn't wait to see if Cooper had anything else to add. Call him rude; call him a coward. He just headed around the man aiming straight for his truck.

He'd stepped forward with Anthony last year because it had been the right thing to do. Whether he liked it or not, he'd known he wasn't the boy's father. But that didn't mean he wanted to stand around in a parking lot with Anthony's rightful father shooting the breeze.

Except for the flowers, he dumped his purchases into the basket, and drove to the airport.

Emily was already there by the time he turned into the parking lot. He pulled into the closest spot to hers and climbed out, lifting his hand in a wave.

She was standing next to her fancy rental car, shading her eyes with her hand, her lips curved in a slight smile. "Good morning," she called.

"Morning." He grabbed his flight bag and the basket off the other seat. The knot in his chest disappeared as he headed toward her. She wasn't wearing her glasses and the top she had on reminded him vaguely of the ones the waitresses wore at Red—ruffled around the top and slipping off one shoulder—only hers was white and paired with a pair of blue jeans.

He'd never seen her in blue jeans.

She'd also left her hair loose and it drifted long and silky straight around her arms.

She looked carefree and pretty and so damn approachable he could almost forget who she was.

"Isn't it a beautiful day?" She lifted her chin toward the sky, closing her eyes like she was receiving the sun's kiss.

His hand tightened on the wooden handles of the basket. "Beautiful," he agreed gruffly.

Her lashes lifted and color suffused her cheeks.

"Here." He abruptly held out the daisies. "These are for you."

Her fingers brushed his as she slowly took the cellophane-wrapped bundle. "They're lovely."

He shrugged, thinking he'd have been better off to leave the flowers in his truck. She'd have never needed to know about them. "They're just a few daisies," he dismissed.

"But they're still daisies." She'd lifted the flowers to her nose and she eyed him over the sunny white blooms, giving a shrug of her own that seemed to match his in awkwardness. "No one has ever given me daisies before," she said.

"No man has given you flowers before." He didn't believe it for a second.

"Not daisies." She traced her fingertip over the petals and gave him a surprisingly shy smile. "And they're my favorite. Thank you."

And then he wished he'd bought out the entire bucket of them just so he could see that smile again. "You're welcome."

She gestured toward the basket. "Is that a picnic basket?"

"You said you liked Sunday afternoon picnics."

"I did. I do." Her eyes met his, then skittered away. "At least I believe that I will. Since this is another first."

He took a step toward her before he even realized what he was doing and he sharply reined in the urge to kiss her. Not because he didn't want to. He did.

But the parking lot was busy with people coming and going. He didn't particularly want to give Tanner's other employees and the customers something like this to gossip about.

"It's a first for me, too," he told her. He lifted the basket a few inches. "Had to borrow this from Mrs. Sheckley. It weighs more than it should just because of the brownies she included."

He wouldn't have thought it possible, but Emily's expression softened even more. She suddenly stepped forward, nearly squashing the flowers between their bodies as she reached up to press her lips against his.

The kiss was fleeting.

Not long enough at all for him to turn it back on her, to deepen it and damn who might see.

Then she was settling back on the heels of her strappy sandals and giving him that shy look all over again. "You make it very hard for me to resist you."

Something unfamiliar squeezed through his chest and he curled his fingers more tightly around the basket handle. "Likewise."

Her smile widened. She bent her head over the flowers, grazing the blooms against her cheek. "So, um, where are we going to fly to? Or do we just go," she twirled her finger in the air, "around in circles?"

"There's a place about an hour away." He

touched her elbow, setting off toward the hangar. "Tanner turned me on to it after I'd soloed. It's an old airfield that runs right next to a little creek."

"Sounds nice."

"Peaceful, anyway." He'd spent a lot of time sitting on the banks of that creek after Anthony's true paternity had been finally determined. But that wasn't why he'd chosen the spot today.

That was because of much simpler reasons. Close enough for a day trip. And pretty enough to share with Emily.

He aimed for the office door. "You want me to find something to stick the flowers in?"

"The stems are in water already. See?" She held up the bouquet. And sure enough, inside the cellophane wrapper, each stem was stuck in a clear little tube filled with liquid. He hadn't even noticed. When she lowered the bouquet again, she held it close against her chest. As if she didn't want to let loose of them.

He felt that unfamiliar, squeezing sensation inside his chest again but kept his brain focused on the tasks at hand. He shifted course a little, away from the office. "Then we can head on out to the plane." He shot her a quick look. "You nervous?"

Was she nervous? Emily thought about it as she quickened her step, keeping up with Max as they rounded one side of the hangar. "Maybe a little," she admitted. "Not because I don't trust you or anything," she added quickly. "Tanner says you're a really safe pilot."

Max glanced at her. His blue eyes looked amused. "Checked with the boss, did you?"

"No." She couldn't seem to stop touching the velvety-soft daisy petals. "But he and Jordana were over at the house this morning having an early breakfast with us. And I, um, happened to mention our plans."

She'd earned an arch look from Wendy as a result, too, who'd gone on to tell the others just how late it had been when Emily arrived home after her date with Max. She'd known exactly, because she'd been up with a restless MaryAnne.

Emily had kicked Wendy beneath the table before she could also share just how disheveled she'd looked when Max had dropped her off.

"You know. How you're giving me some real-time experience with flying. Market research." She was in danger of babbling and quickly shut her mouth.

"Then what are you nervous about?"

About spending more time with him?

About his reaction if she were to tell him that she was only days away from learning whether or not she was pregnant, courtesy of an anonymous donor?

"I've never been on such a small plane," she said, instead. Which was certainly true.

"The girl we're taking up is steady as a rock. We've flown together a lot. But, if you hate it, say the word and I'll turn around and land."

She was pretty sure she wasn't going to hate it.

Not when she'd be sitting next to him.

Instead of going into the hangar, which she'd sort of expected, they crossed the tarmac some distance away, finally coming to a small white-and-green plane with a propeller on its nose, an overhead wing, and a large set of numbers painted on the side. Max went straight to one side of the plane, ducked slightly beneath the wing and pulled open the passenger-side door. He set the picnic basket and the same sort of flight bag that she'd seen Tanner use inside the plane, then turned back to her.

He held out his hand toward her. "You ready?"

He had a pair of aviator sunglasses tucked

in his navy blue T-shirt and his brown hair was a little shaggy, falling over his forehead. His expression was clear, the smile on his lips slightly crooked. And she felt her heart skitter around inside her chest.

She moistened her lips. Walked over to him, and put her hand in his. "I'm ready."

She just wasn't entirely sure if she meant she was ready for the plane ride, or for him.

Chapter 8

Emily had traveled by air countless times in her life. Commercial jetliners. Chartered, executive jets. But every time, it had been just a means to an end. A way of getting from here to there.

Sitting on the worn leather seat next to Max as he piloted the small plane, she wasn't sure if she was more fascinated by the Texas landscape below them, or by Max himself.

He was so obviously in his element and it was sheer pleasure to watch him.

Before they'd taken off, he'd walked around the plane, checking this, checking that. Then he'd done the same thing while inside the plane before sticking his head out the window and yelling "Clear!" After a moment, the propeller had spun a few times, slowly at first, then faster and faster until it was a blur in front of the plane. The takeoff itself had been wholly exhilarating. Emily had laughed right out loud when she'd felt the little craft escape the hold of the runway and whoosh up into the air.

They'd been flying about an hour—an unexpectedly tranquil hour—when Max treated her to another rush. Barreling downward toward an impossibly narrow runway that was stuck out in the tall grass in what seemed the absolute middle of nowhere. She felt the pull of gravity as they smoothly landed, the press of motion against her as Max corralled the speeding plane down the runway and, in her opinion, masterfully slowed to a quiet, gentle stop well before they ran out of pavement.

She exhaled. Pressed her palm against her thundering heart and looked around as Max taxied the plane away from the runway and onto the field between it and the trees. Aside from the runway—faded and sprouting grass among the cracks—there was only one small building, a truck that she assumed carried fuel and a windsock blowing from a tall post. On the other side of the runway, she could see glimpses of the creek, glimmering beyond a stand of trees.

She didn't know where they were. Didn't particularly care. It felt like they were the only two people on earth right there, and she was simply enchanted.

"So," Max cut the plane's engine and the propeller slowly stopped spinning, "what'd you think?"

"I think it was fabulous." She turned from the side window to look at him. She still held her daisies on her lap. "And I think you should be flying all the time."

His lips tilted. "Yeah, but this little hobby doesn't pay the bills. And it creates a bunch of new ones." He reached right over her and un-latched the door beside her, then straightened to push open his own. After unfastening his safety belt, he climbed out, grabbing a set of wheel chocks from the cargo area behind the seats as he went. "Sit tight. I'll come around and help you out."

He climbed out and disappeared from view, reappearing a few moments later at her door. He pulled it open, and took her flowers in one hand while he held her hand securely in his other until she'd climbed out. Once she was safely on the ground, he handed her the flowers again and reached back into the plane to retrieve the picnic basket.

Then he tucked his hand under her elbow, ducked his head again to clear the wing and headed toward the trees. The long, soft grass tickled her feet through her strappy sandals and she couldn't help swinging her foot through it as if she were kicking a ball.

"Grass tickles," she told Max when he shot her a glance over the tops of his sunglasses.

His smile widened, obviously amused. "One of those simple pleasures of yours?"

"Exactly."

He let go of her elbow, gesturing toward the trees. "Well, knock yourself out, baby. Kick away."

Knowing the endearment didn't mean anything didn't stop her from latching on to it, and she felt as if her face might split from the smile she couldn't seem to tame. "Well, now I can't," she complained lightly. "Because I'll feel silly."

"Too bad. I was getting a good image in my head of what you must have looked like as a little girl. Sort of hoping you'd start turning cartwheels or something."

She let out a soft laugh. "Even as a little girl, I couldn't turn a cartwheel to save my life. I was a complete, bossy little geek." She didn't know what possessed her, but she stuck out her hands, planting them in the thick grass and threw her legs over in a wholly pathetic cartwheel. But her heart was light and she didn't care if she looked ridiculous. Particularly when she straightened and he was smiling indulgently. "Still am a geek," she said breathlessly.

"Not bossy?"

She grinned. "Not unless I'm in the office."

"Then that just leaves you being the prettiest geek I've ever met."

Her heart skittered around as if she'd just attempted another cartwheel. "You wouldn't have thought so when I had braces to go with these glasses and was head of the debate team in junior high."

"Don't underestimate the sexual appeal of a teenage girl in braces to a teenage boy," he countered. They'd reached the trees and he grabbed her hand, his fingers threading through hers as he took the lead.

Emily was glad to follow behind him. It gave her a chance to pull in a deep, soundless breath. And to admire the hind view of him.

But they were soon beyond the thickest part of the trees as the area opened up again into a narrow, pretty meadow running directly beside the creek bed. The sun was bright and warm overhead, the grass smelled sweet and she was utterly charmed.

Max set down the picnic basket and opened the lid to pull out a red-and-black plaid blanket, which he flipped open on the ground. He anchored one corner with the basket, and the other with Mrs. Sheckley's bag of brownies. "You going to stand there, or come sit?"

She kicked off her sandals, curling her bare toes into the cushiony grass. "For someone with no picnic experience," she told him, "this looks sort of magazine perfect."

"Thank Mrs. Sheckley for that, too." He sat down on the blanket. "She and Mr. Sheckley evidently went on a lot of picnics." His teeth flashed in a quick grin. "She actually told me her oldest son and her youngest daughter were both conceived while picnicking."

Emily nearly choked. "On *that* blanket?"

He chuckled. "Not this one. It was brand-new. Saw it come out of her closet, still wrapped." He reached into the picnic basket and pulled out two bottles. One lemonade, one water. "Which one? Got plenty of both."

She stepped onto the soft blanket and sat down on her folded legs. She took the water and twisted it open. "Thanks."

He opened his lemonade and clinked the plastic bottle against hers. "Here's to our first picnic."

Which only had her wondering if there'd be more than one. Afraid her thoughts would show on her face, she sipped the water and glanced over at the creek. "How many times have you been out here?"

"Probably a dozen." He stretched out his legs and leaned down on one bent arm. "Give or take."

Her fingertip slid beneath the edge of the paper label on the water bottle. "Ever bring anyone?"

He was silent for a beat. "Another woman, you mean?"

Her cheeks heated.

His dimple flashed. "No other women," he finally said. "Nobody else, period."

She set the flowers on the blanket beside her before twisting her legs from beneath her and hugged her knees to her chest. She wished he'd take off the sunglasses so she could see his eyes. "So you'd just fly out here, land and take off again right back to Red Rock?"

"Sometimes. Most times I'd sit here on the ground and stare at the creek."

As lovely as the spot was, it seemed like

a place meant to be shared. But then, maybe that was the closet-romantic she'd never known existed inside her that was talking. "Sounds lonely."

He slowly shook his head. "Couple times I felt like this place and that plane back there were the only things keeping me sane."

"Because of Anthony?" She held her breath the second the question escaped.

He sipped his lemonade, taking a nerve-racking amount of time before responding. "I figured it was too much to expect you not to have heard about all that."

She started breathing again. Cautiously. "Wendy told me a little." She shook her head once. "I shouldn't have brought it up."

"Why?"

She dashed her hair away from her cheek. "Because it's your business. If you wanted to share it, you would."

"So if I don't say another word about him, you're okay with that?"

Her lips parted, ready to agree. But the truth made her hesitate. "If you wanted to talk about him, I'd be happy to listen. But I'll respect your right to privacy," she finally said. "We certainly don't have to exchange our deepest secrets for us to enjoy each other's company."

In fact, she knew it was probably better if they didn't. She didn't want anything ruining this time with him yet and she could imagine how fast and far he'd run once she shared her motherhood intentions.

He took another long sip of his lemonade. "You scare the hell out of me, you know that? Aside from my sister, you must be the most honest person I've ever encountered."

Her conscience pinched. "I don't know about that. I just know that I, well... I like you, Max. That's all." She did like him. She liked the way she felt when she was with him.

He pulled off his sunglasses and tossed them on the blanket. His eyes were narrowed against the sunlight as he looked at her, but she could still make out the clear, pale blue as his gaze captured hers. "That's *all?*"

Her heart surged straight up her throat. "You know that's not all. But...but nothing's changed since the other night. Tanner is still my brother-in-law. And judging by the way he and Jordana are joined at the hip, I don't think that's likely to change anytime this millennium."

Whatever she'd expected from Max, it wasn't the smile he gave. "He is pretty gung ho over her and that baby she's carrying."

She shifted again until she was sitting cross-legged. "I still can't believe both of my little sisters are even married, much less starting families already." She slid a single daisy out from the bunch. "I used to think Wendy was so wild. And Jordana—" She twirled the stem between her fingers. "Jordana was just the opposite. For a while she was terminally shy."

"And you were somewhere in between."

"Closer to Jordana's shy end than Wendy's confident one."

He gave a faint snort. "Please. You're confident as hell."

"About work, yes. But anything else in life?" She made a face and shook her head. "Not so much. Advertising is a lot easier than personal relationships. But even when it comes to my career, I've only ever worked at FortuneSouth. Maybe I just got where I am there because of nepotism. My father's the one that hired me, after all."

"He make a habit of hiring unqualified people?" Max didn't wait for her to answer before he shook his head. "I've read up on FortuneSouth. Companies don't get that successful if there are incompetent people running things."

She watched him from beneath her lashes. "You checked up on the company?"

He suddenly rolled onto his stomach, bringing him within inches of her knees, and he plucked the flower stem out of her fingers. "I checked up on *you*." He touched the daisy to her chin. "You've won advertising awards. I doubt they had anything to do with nepotism. But you didn't tell Tanner to take a flying leap when he asked you to meet with me."

"Tanner's family. Of course I wasn't going to turn him down. And I was the one to butt my nose in anyway, when I mentioned that his current website could use some jazzing up." She pressed her lips together. "I just didn't expect what I found."

One of Max's eyebrows went up when she hesitated.

"You," she finished simply. She spread her hands, palms up. "I don't make a habit of throwing myself at anyone but I've done just that, more than once, with you. Even though I know you don't want to go...you know... *there*."

"Yeah, I was really putting up a fight the other night when Mrs. Sheckley interrupted." His voice dropped a notch, heavy with irony. "Because I didn't want to go...you know... *there*."

She grimaced. "You see? Advertising, good. Personal relationships, bad."

"That makes two of us, then, when it comes to relationships. I've never had a single one that lasted." He suddenly broke the head of the daisy off, leaving only a few inches of stem attached and reached up to tuck it behind her ear. "Come on." He sat up and began removing his well-worn athletic shoes and socks. "It's getting hot. You wanna wade in the creek?"

"Is it okay to leave our things here?"

"Sure," he assured carelessly. "Nobody's ever around."

"Not even over at that little building by the runway?"

He shook his head. "There's a guy who comes if you call him for assistance. Otherwise, we're all alone."

She absorbed that. "Creek sounds good." She had to push out the words since her throat had gone dry.

He extended his hand, and she took it, letting him pull her to her own feet. Without releasing her, he turned and aimed for the creek. "Be careful," he warned when they reached the water's edge. "It's not deep but the rocks are slippery." He let go of her hand and rolled up the legs of his jeans.

Emily tried not to stare too hard at the muscular calves he revealed. Or at his bare feet. She'd never considered how sexy a man's feet could be, but Max's definitely were.

She quickly rolled up her own jeans and stepped into the cool water, realizing immediately that Max hadn't exaggerated the slipperiness of the rocky surface when she pitched forward.

Max's arm caught her around the waist, hauling her upright. "Careful."

She clutched his hair-roughened forearm, wholly conscious of the heat of his body so close to hers. "Thanks. I'm, uh, I'm good."

He waited a moment longer, as if he weren't quite convinced, but then his arm loosened and fell away. He took her hand. "Step where I step." He looked over his shoulder at her to see that she did just that as he waded through the water.

She realized he was heading closer to the center of the creek when the water gurgled around her calves rather than her ankles. The bottom of the creek also was much smoother there. Sandier. Less rocky and considerably easier to walk on. "I've never done this, either," she told him.

"Are you a virgin, too?"

Shock rippled down her spine. "What?"

He looked over his shoulder, giving her a wicked grin that could have caused angels to willingly topple. "Just checking what else might be a first."

Despite herself, she laughed. Rolled her eyes. "Not that," she assured. Though considering the other night, even that unfinished taste with him eclipsed anything she'd experienced before. "You?" She turned the question around quickly.

He gave a bark of laughter. "That happened a helluva long time ago. Courtesy of Stacey Fletcher, who sat next to me in eighth grade biology." He faced forward again. "She had braces," he added.

Emily leaned down and scooped up water in her hand, flicking it at his head. "You're making that up. Eighth grade? You were a child!"

He held up his other hand, three fingers extended tightly. "Scout's honor."

"Were you a Boy Scout?"

"Not even close. But it's still the truth." He dropped his hand, only to stop and point off to the other side of the creek. "Look." His voice was soft.

She followed his finger and saw three deer quietly grazing in the shade of the trees. But even as she and Max went still, Emily stopping behind him so closely that her hands came to rest on his back, one of the animals lifted its head and stared at them.

Then, after a long, motionless moment, all three turned as one and bounded away, their tan hides disappearing among the trees.

Emily sighed happily and resisted the urge to rest her cheek on Max's back. "Do you hunt?"

"Never much saw the appeal." He looked back at her. "Don't have an issue with people who do, particularly, though. You?"

"My father will hunt if he can somehow combine a business deal with it. He's never invited me along."

"Did you want him to?"

"I wanted to be included in anything that would get him to care that I was around," she said truthfully. "But I'm a girl. And hunting—along with golf and pool and cigar clubs, which I'm also not interested in—are for boys only as far as he's concerned. So I knew I'd never have to be faced with that particular choice." She looked over to the trees the deer had disappeared into. "Fortunately."

He took her hand in his again, and started

wading forward once more. "What about your mom?"

"If John Michael Fortune is the quintessential Southern business genius, then Virginia Alice Fortune is the quintessential Southern little woman." She swished her feet in the chilly water, her gaze returning to Max's back in front of her. "All she ever wanted in her life was a pretty home and a passel of kids and she's a wonderful mother. But she positively dotes on my father."

"Sounds like you think that's a bad thing."

"No." She thought about it. Emily had always believed her mother was rather overshadowed by John Michael, who'd always seemed larger than life, and plenty domineering. He expected everyone around him to toe his line. "I just wish that he'd dote on her a little in return."

"Maybe he does when you're not around to see it. How long have they been married?"

"Long enough to raise six children." Her gaze followed the slightly strained shoulder seam of his T-shirt down to the tanned biceps that bulged against his short sleeve. "Whatever keeps them together works for them, I guess."

"I've been told it's love that's supposed to do that."

"Love. Money. Good old-fashioned Southern propriety. Maybe all three. What about your parents?" His "love" comment had sounded distinctly jaded.

"My dad walked out on us when Kirsten and I were kids and my mom died a while back."

Understanding hit. "I'm sorry."

"No reason." The creek narrowed even more as they came upon several large boulders, and he stepped out of the water on the other side, turning back to grab her other hand and guide her up beside him.

"It must have been hard, though."

"Harder on Kirsten. She thought it was up to her to finish raising me after Mom died. I didn't make that very easy for her."

Emily thought about the woman they'd run into at Red. "Kirsten can't be that much older than you."

"Just two years." He sat down on one of the enormous boulders and tugged Emily forward, covering her hips with his hands and pulling her right down onto his lap. "I told you I was a hellion. If anyone said turn right, I'd have to go left, just to prove that I could."

Her brains were suddenly scrambled. She stared into Max's face, only inches from hers, feeling the hard muscles of his thighs beneath her. "And now?" Her voice sounded faint.

"Now, I care a little more about making the right turns for me."

She swallowed. He had a nearly invisible scar just below the corner of his right eye that she hadn't noticed before. One portion of her addled brain wondered if he'd gotten it during his hellion years. "What sort of turn am I?"

His hands drifted up her back, his fingertips seeming to find every indentation of her spine. "You're an entire road map all on your own."

Shivers danced under her skin wherever he touched. She shifted and rested her hands on his shoulders. "Is that good or bad?"

"I've always loved a good road trip."

She felt her cheeks turn hot even though something inside her was dancing a little jig.

He laughed softly. His fingers moved lightly over her bare shoulder, setting off shivers. "You're not wearing your glasses today."

"I mostly need them for reading and computer work." She wouldn't admit to the real reason she'd left them tucked inside her purse—that she didn't want to feel like a bespectacled geek that day. She wanted to feel feminine. And sexy. Which was the same reason she'd borrowed the blouse from Wendy.

"You're not wearing anything under this shirt, either, are you?"

It wasn't really a question. She shook her head, anyway, feeling her skin turn even warmer.

His gaze was focused on his hand as he traced the wide, elasticized neckline across her collarbone to the other side. Slowly nudged it down until it matched the other side, situated just below the point of her shoulder. "And if I wanted to pull it down more?"

She could barely breathe. "Even though it's...not smart?"

His thumb brushed over her bare shoulder, back and forth in a mesmerizing way. He gave a slow, steady nod. "Even though."

She moistened her lips. "I've never done anything like this."

"Out in the open, you mean?" His hand glided down, leaving her blouse in place. She was unaccountably disappointed. Until his palm grazed over her breast.

She sucked in an audibly sharp breath. "Right. Open." She sounded like a breathless idiot and couldn't do a thing to change it. Beneath the crisp cotton separating his palm from her, her nipple felt achingly tight, exquisitely sensitive.

His gaze found hers. "Does that bother you?"

She laughed weakly. She might as well have been ice cream melting under the sunlight. "Nothing seems to bother me much when it comes to you."

He smiled slightly. His fingertips curled, sliding a few inches beneath the elastic neckline.

She held her breath.

But still he didn't pull down the top. "Are you on the pill?"

She opened her mouth. Why hadn't she anticipated this?

Because she was more used to dealing with her staffers than she was with situations like this. That's why.

And yet, she wasn't going to lie about it. "No."

"Good thing I came prepared then," he murmured and finally, steadily pulled down the blouse until the elastic was caught over the crests of her breasts.

Her mind swam. The sun was hot on her back but it was nothing compared to the heat growing inside her. "Prepared?"

"Condom." He caught her lips with his in a soft, biting little kiss that made her famished for more. "We're too old to take stupid chances."

If she weren't in danger of dissolving right over him, she would have cried at the irony. "Are you going to make love to me, or keep talking?"

He laughed softly. Kissed the point of one shoulder. Then the other. And still he didn't make that elastic budge. "So, the bossy Emily rears her head after all."

Shudders worked down her spine. "Not bossy," she said huskily. "Just desperate." She twisted her head around until she found his mouth with hers. "Which is all your doing, anyway," she accused against his lips.

"And you're going to be my undoing," he returned, then opened his mouth over hers.

Colors burst behind her eyes as he kissed her.

She forgot about the hot sun, about the open air, about the creek and the trees and the deer. She forgot everything but Max. The taste of him. The feel of him. She couldn't get enough.

Wasn't sure she'd ever get enough.

He finally lifted his head, his breath as harsh as hers. He dragged the elastic over her hypersensitive nipples, all the way down to her waist, effectively trapping her arms as well, and lowered his head, catching first one peak in his mouth, and then the other.

Emily's head fell back heavily. His arm was behind her back, arching her into him and her hands curled into fists. She moaned, the exquisite sensation of his mouth on her nearly more than she could bear.

Then his kiss burned from her breasts back up to her mouth again. "We should go back to the picnic spot," he said roughly. "The blanket—"

She pressed her mouth against his neck. Tasted the salt of his sweat. She tugged at the bottom of his T-shirt with her trapped hands. "Too far. I can't wait."

He gave a muffled laugh. He pulled the sleeves of her blouse down until her arms were free, then jerked his own shirt right off and pitched it to the ground, not seeming to care that it dragged in the creek.

Hardly believing that she could be so bold, she reached between them and fumbled with his belt, her eyes greedily taking in the sight of the dark hair arrowing down his hard, bare chest. "You, uh, you always carry condoms?"

"Not in years." He worked at her jeans, too, and was much more efficient at it than she was, pulling them down her hips before she'd even managed to undo his belt. "Started again just this morning. Lift."

She lifted her rear and he tugged her jeans down even more, somehow managing to pull them and his own clear of their legs without dumping either one of them into the creek. He rescued a little packet from his pocket before tossing his jeans aside.

And then, despite the sun, Emily shivered as he pulled her back down onto his lap, her legs straddling him. A slight shift of her hips, a quick arch against him, and she'd be able to take him, every straining, hard, beautiful inch of him, inside.

She trembled. "Hurry." If he didn't, she was afraid she would. Not because of the consequences she could be inviting if her appointment the other day hadn't been successful, but because she ached, positively ached, to have nothing between them.

He rapidly ripped open the packet and sheathed himself. Then his hands closed over her hips, tilting her against him and she cried out sharply as he sank deep inside her. Stretching. Filling.

He immediately stilled, groaning, the sound low and fierce and wholly thrilling. "Are you okay?"

She nodded, too overcome for words, and pressed her open mouth against the hard bulge of his tanned shoulder. "It's just been a while," she gasped. "Don't stop." Even as she said it, she felt him surge against the very heart of her.

His fingers flexed against her derriere. "I don't think I could if I wanted to." His breath rasped against her ear. "And I don't want to."

Thank goodness. She heard a keening sound come from her throat as, with every moment, the entire world shrank down to just the two of them, spiraling ever downward, right inside her, more and more tightly. Her fingers dug into Max's back as control spun out of her grasp. She gasped his name, suddenly afraid of losing herself completely in the catapult of sensation.

As if he'd read her mind, his fierce grip suddenly eased. Slowed. His palm slid up her spine. Cradled her neck. "It's okay," he murmured. His mouth found hers and he kissed her slowly. Impossibly gentle.

She didn't know why. But tears suddenly burned from the corners of her eyes. He caught them with his thumbs. Pressed her eyes closed with a kiss as light as a wish.

"I've got you, Emily." He rocked slowly, steadily, stealing her breath all over again. "It's okay. Just let yourself go, baby," he whispered. "I'll be right with you." He threaded his fingers through her hair, urging her head back until she felt the sun on her face and his kiss on her throat.

Emily opened her eyes. Stared blindly up at the cloudless sky that was almost as perfect a blue as Max's eyes, and felt more pleasure than she'd known existed blossoming inside every fiber of her being.

He exhaled roughly, his hands still rigidly gentle even as she felt him surge more deeply, impossibly, inside her.

Then suddenly, she was there.

And nothing existed except that pulse of her very soul against his—an endless perfection that hurtled her off the edge of the cliff, weightless and free—with only Max there to cradle her as they landed.

Chapter 9

Eventually, they made their way back to their picnic spot the same way they'd come, through the creek.

And just as Max had promised, not a single thing had changed in their absence.

Only she was the one to feel wholly changed.

And because she did, she took refuge in the practical. The mundane. She quickly opened the picnic basket and found sandwiches tucked neatly against a cold pack. She held them up. "Does it matter which?"

Max hadn't put on his wet shirt again, and he spread it out on the grass before sitting beside her on the blanket. He looked more closely at the paper-wrapped bundles. "This one's ham. That's turkey. Take your pick."

She handed him the ham and reached back into the basket. She was surprised at how well-equipped it was, right down to glass-looking acrylic wineglasses. "Kudos to Mrs. Sheckley," she said, pulling them out, along with crisp, white fabric napkins. "Here." She handed Max a napkin and then poured lemonade into the two glasses.

"To our first picnic." He took one of the glasses and clinked it against hers. His gaze was lazy. Amused and satisfied and so, so very attractive. "And other firsts."

She had no right to feel heat pool inside her again, not yet. Not so soon.

But she did. And it was dizzying.

She took a sip of lemonade and carefully set the glass aside, balancing it against her knee, and unwrapped her sandwich. "Will it be hard passing the test for your instrument rating?"

He smiled slightly as if he were perfectly aware of her predicament. "Tests. I've already passed the written exam. Next week'll be the practical, which has an oral component and an actual flight exam."

"Sounds complicated. I always hated tests

when I was in school. Didn't matter how well prepared I was, I always worried."

"On the other hand, I avoided tests back then by not taking them at all." He leaned back against the picnic basket and studied the sandwich in his hand. "Didn't start caring about passing anything until I finally got my GED and started paying for online college courses."

"You've also been taking college courses? Along with flying?" She stared at him, finally managing to overlook the starving sexual monster he'd seemed to create of her. "Where do you find the time?"

"Don't need a lot of sleep."

"I guess not." She could hardly imagine it. While she'd been in college, she'd interned— barely part-time—at FortuneSouth and had had all of her expenses paid by her father.

"Once I started my instrument rating, I had to lay off the online courses. Took too much time and money."

"What were you taking?"

"Business." He made a face. "English. Pretty much the remedial version since that was about my least favorite subject in school."

"What was your favorite subject?"

"Girls," he said immediately.

She flicked the corner of her napkin at him. "Seriously."

"I dunno. Science I guess."

"Right. Biology. I remember."

He grinned. "There were other sciences. I remember building a few rockets. One of the few times I ever earned As."

"So you had a thing for air travel even then."

His face was relaxed, his dimple flashing. "Who knew?"

"So what was it?" She'd finished her sandwich and hadn't even realized it, and still hungry, she poked inside the basket and discovered a small bag of potato chips. She tore it open and sank her teeth into one of the salty crisps with relish. "The flying bug that ended up biting you?"

"I was afraid I'd start drinking again after I turned Anthony over to the authorities."

She went still.

"Not long after I gave him up, I was driving to the old bar where I'd always hung." His voice was casual, though she didn't buy it for a second. "Just wanted to get my hands around a bottle of whiskey and forget everything."

She was almost afraid to speak for fear that he'd stop. "What happened?"

"Gary—my first instructor—was tending at the bar. His son Jack owns the place."

Her lips parted.

"I ordered the shot and that old man just took one look at my face and said, 'Son, what you need isn't here.'" Max's gaze met hers. "I reached over to grab the booze anyway and he grabbed my shirt." He fisted his hand, holding it against his throat. "Right here. And even though I was taller, younger and outweighed him, he pulled me out of the bar, pushed me back in my car and gave me a business card. Told me to get my head on straight and give him a call. First lesson was on him."

"What'd you do?"

"Drove to a different bar. Put back more shots of whiskey than I can remember and nearly drove myself into a tree." His gaze didn't shirk from hers. "I was lucky I didn't end up killing someone."

"Including yourself," she managed faintly.

His lips twisted. "That, too. I cleaned up. Sobered up. I was lucky that I'd never been picked up for DUI. And then I went out and took that first free flying lesson."

"And you were hooked," she finished. "How did Gary know that's what you needed?"

"Because he'd been there himself."

She absorbed that. Thank heaven for Gary. As far as she was concerned, he'd started earning his wings before he'd ever left this life. "And now?" She lifted the stemmed glass of lemonade. "You're not tempted?"

"I won't lie. Sometimes I think I am. But—" he shook his head "—it's just not worth it. I can look in my mirror these days and not hate the guy staring back."

"I think the guy staring back is quite remarkable."

Max felt his neck get hot. He hadn't been asking for her praise, just had wanted her to know where he came from. He managed a rakish grin. "That's just because I succeeded in stripping you naked while sitting on a boulder."

As he'd hoped, Emily's cheeks went red. Her lashes swept down and she shoved a potato chip between her soft, pink lips. "What happened after the free lesson? Is that when you started doing odd jobs for Tanner?"

He nodded. "In exchange for the fees that would have easily taken me five times as long to afford."

"So you had a plan," she murmured. "And you worked the plan."

"Yeah," he agreed slowly. "I guess you could put it that way."

"How far does the plan extend?" Obviously finished with the chips, she dusted her fingers on her napkin and handed him the bag to finish. "Just through getting your instrument rating?"

He narrowed his eyes. "What are you trying to get at?"

She lifted her shoulder in a casual move that he didn't buy for a second. "Nothing. It just seems a shame not to continue pursuing something you clearly love."

"Is that what you always do? Pursue the things you love?"

She turned and looked at the creek, presenting him with the lines of her perfect profile. "I...pursue the things that I know I want," she said.

"Isn't that the same thing?"

"I'm not sure." She finally looked back at him, her gaze meeting his only to flick away again. "Probably."

He watched her for a moment. "What is it that's really keeping you in Red Rock, Emily? What is it that *you're* pursuing?"

"Do you remember what you said to me at the airport that day? When the tornado hit?"

He didn't have to work hard to recall the horror of that day. Or the impact he'd felt when she'd looked up at him. But what he'd specifically said? "You were pinned under a rack of metal chairs and a helluva lot of other debris, I remember that. I told you they were going to get you out."

"You also told me I had a future just waiting for me to live."

"Did I?" He pinched his earlobe, more clearly remembering that he'd been trying to say something, anything, encouraging to a terrified woman. "I remember thinking you had the prettiest green eyes I'd ever seen."

She smiled slightly, seeming to lose some of whatever tension had gripped her. "Even though I was covered in dirt?"

"Even though."

"Well, you did say it." Her slender fingers toyed with the stem of her glass. "To me, it felt like you'd been reading my mind. But even if you weren't, your words mattered. That day changed my life," she said simply. "It brought into very clear focus how little everything I'd done up to that point actually counted. My career. FortuneSouth." She shook her head. "That's what I've been good at, but in the end, it's not what really matters."

"Which is what? Relationships, I suppose."

"Relationships. Friends. Family." She hesitated, her gaze glancing over his yet again. "Children."

"Well, nothing against relationships." He crumpled the potato chip bag he'd emptied and reached out to grab the picnic basket. "Or family or friends. But children definitely aren't in the cards for me. Anthony proved that." He found the enormous chocolate bar he'd packed and held it up. "Chocolate. The richest, most sinful-looking kind I could think of to bring to a picnic."

She barely glanced at the candy. "Just because Anthony isn't yours biologically doesn't mean you can't have a relationship with him." He gave her a look and she flushed. "Wendy told me that even though you've had opportunities, you've steadfastly refused to see him."

"Wendy talks a lot."

"She's my sister," she defended. "She's lived in Red Rock longer than me. I asked about you and things…came up."

"And Lily Fortune is related to you," he concluded. He still got a paycheck from the woman even though they were becoming more and more infrequent due to the decreasing hours he'd been putting in working at the ranch. She'd never been anything but kind to him, but he knew the fact that he'd refused her attempts to arrange a meeting with Anthony had to have come directly from her. His sister knew about it, naturally, but he was fairly certain that Kirsten wouldn't have blabbed his personal business to anyone, even Wendy Fortune Mendoza.

"It's all water under the bridge," he said, though it wasn't entirely true. "Anthony's got his real father now and a stepmother who loves him as if she'd given birth to him, herself. He's got everything he deserves. Will continue to have everything he deserves."

Emily's brows pulled together. Her eyes were filled with shadow. "I can tell that you miss him, though. What about what you deserve?"

He didn't want anything ruining his afternoon with Emily. "The only one deserving anything right here is you, who won that bet of mine when we were at Red, fair and square. The stakes were dessert." He peeled the thick, glossy paper away from one end of the chocolate bar and broke off a piece. "Sinful, rich and chocolate, I believe you said." The warm afternoon had already begun to soften the chocolate and between his fingers, it grew even softer.

He leaned closer to Emily. "Open up and take your winnings."

She hesitated for a moment. Then she exhaled and obeyed.

He nudged the chocolate past her pearly white teeth and her lips closed, catching the tip of his thumb, as well.

A bolt of heat shot straight down his spine.

The shadows in her eyes shifted and her lashes fell, but not quickly enough for him miss the way her pupils dilated.

He slowly pulled his hand away. Her tongue snuck out, swiping over her lower lip, leaving it shining and damnably tempting and he scooped his hand through her silky hair, tugging her to him to cover her mouth with his.

She made a soft sound, her hands splaying against his chest as she kissed him back, just as hungrily. He could taste the chocolate on her tongue, smell the sun in her hair. And even though they'd just made love, he wanted her all over again.

He groaned. Kissed her hard and set her away from him. "Stop tempting me."

Her eyes had turned drowsy and color spiked in her cheeks. "Why?"

"Because I only had one condom."

"If you'd been a Boy Scout, maybe you'd have come prepared with more than one."

He gave a bark of laughter, grabbed her close and kissed her again, twisting her right around until she lay on the blanket. Her hair spread wildly around her shoulders, looking nearly white against the red-and-black plaid. "Who knew my misspent youth would one day lead to this particularly frustrating moment?"

She giggled and the sound was so unexpected coming from her that he could only laugh again. And then he could only kiss her again. And know that the taste of *her* was a lot more addictive than chocolate.

When he lifted his head again, her eyes seemed to glow as she stared up at him. He could see her pulse beating at the base of her throat and he slowly lowered his head, pressing his lips right there, feeling the quick swallow she gave, the faint, breathy sound that rose in her throat.

"Max," she whispered. "You said we couldn't…couldn't—"

"Take a chance. We won't." And he meant it. He traced the tip of his tongue against her exquisitely fine collarbone. "Just let me touch you." Her legs shifted restlessly against his. She'd dropped the chocolate bar on the blanket and he tossed it carelessly toward the opened picnic basket. "You're so damn beautiful," he muttered, sliding his thigh over hers, mostly to keep her movements from sending him beyond the limits of his control.

But she just made that soft, needy sound again in her throat, the one that raised his blood pressure about a million points, and boldly ran her palm down the front of his abruptly strained jeans. He swallowed an oath and grabbed her hand, pulling it away from him, pressing it back against the blanket. "You're gonna play with fire, there."

"I was trying," she said huskily.

He groaned and rolled right on top of her, hitching her thighs up against his hips. He dragged down the neckline of her blouse again, exposing her pink, pebbled nipples to him, the sky, the sun. "I *really* love this shirt of yours," he muttered.

"I...didn't realize it would be so handy." Her voice was breathless. And then she gasped, her hands sliding over his shoulders, fingers kneading against his flesh like a needy cat when he lowered his mouth to the sweet, warm valley between her breasts.

Her hips arched against him, and even though there were layers of denim between them, he still felt bathed in fire. He shifted, kissing his way down her belly, shoving the white blouse out of his way as he went, tasting the flat little indent of her navel, reaching the low-cut jeans that hugged those racehorse hips and legs of hers so maddeningly. He freed the button and wasn't sure who he was torturing more as he slowly dragged down the zipper.

"Max—"

"I just need to touch you," he murmured. "I won't do more than that, I promise."

She gave a choked laugh. "Is that what you said to your brace-faced friend Stacey?"

"You kidding? She was the one calling the shots that day. I was too damn scared to move."

"I think I'm too scared to move," she admitted. "You make me lose control."

And he loved it that he was the one she'd lose it with. "That's the best part." He slowly pulled her jeans down her hips. Her panties were white and sheer; little more than a few strings and a tiny triangle with a little bow right at the top. For a woman who'd been so buttoned up when they'd first met, she definitely indulged a liking for sexy panties.

He let his fingers drift slowly, tantalizingly, down one string, toward the triangle, and watched, up close and personal, the way her flat stomach seemed to flinch as he grazed his fingertips past the bow, right over her mound.

She inhaled audibly and suddenly twisted her legs, kicking her jeans off the rest of the way. He exhaled, not sure he'd ever felt more relieved than he did knowing she didn't want him to stop.

He bent sharply, kissing the flat of her belly again. Then her knee. The taut curve of her smooth thigh. He let his fingers slide a few inches more, finding her just as hot and slick as she'd felt on the boulder.

She gasped. Closed her hand around his wrist.

But she didn't pull his hand away from that most intimate part of her and when his mouth followed the path his fingers blazed, she cried out his name, her body arching against him. Her hands twisted in his hair and she gave herself over to pleasure.

And it was one of the sweetest things he'd ever known.

"Finish your chocolate," he said a long while later, after she'd finally regained enough energy to dress and he'd regained enough control to stop pacing back and forth alongside the creek while she did. "We're going to have to get back soon." They'd already stayed out longer than he'd planned.

She pulled the enormous chocolate bar out of the picnic basket where he'd tossed it. "You must think I have a really, *really* big appetite." But she broke off another piece and popped it in her mouth, obviously savoring it.

"As long as you keep an appetite for me, eat as much as your heart desires."

"I *desire* you," she murmured, her lips twitching. "But you didn't think ahead well enough to be better prepared."

"Next time I'll have the entire box of condoms," he warned, not entirely joking.

Her cheeks went wildly pink, but her smile didn't fade.

He dragged on his wrinkled shirt and shoes and socks and started packing up the picnic basket, leaving the blanket for last. She wrapped up the rest of the chocolate and tucked it beside the empty glasses, then moved off the blanket to hunt for her sandals that she'd left lying in the grass.

He shook out the blanket and folded it up, but his eyes were on her. Swishing her feet around again in the grass, a daisy in her hand as she searched. The bottom of her jeans was still wet from the creek even though she'd folded them up around her calves, and her hair hung tangled and shining down around her sun-pinkened shoulders.

Then she turned her head, as if feeling his gaze. Her nose was as pink as her shoulders. She smiled at him. "Everything all right?"

Something inside his chest ached. He cleared his throat. "Yeah."

Everything was great.

Except for one problem.

He was falling in love with her.

Flying back to Red Rock felt strangely bittersweet to Emily. The flight back itself was no less exhilarating, but it felt to her as if something perfect and promising was at an end.

And she didn't want it to be.

Max wasn't like anyone she'd ever known. And when she was with him, she felt like she'd never felt before. Let herself behave as she'd never behaved before.

Even now, her body felt liquid and lax, and she still wanted more. More of him. More of everything.

Was it Max himself that caused it all?

Or were her hormones going stark mad because she was already pregnant, just like Wendy had talked about?

She pushed away the thought. It was bad enough that she hadn't told Max anything about her plans yet.

Maybe that made her the worst sort of coward. And if not that, then it was certainly selfish. She wanted her cake and to eat it, too, no matter what she caused along the way...

It made her feel like she possessed the very traits that she'd often blamed her father for possessing.

She listened to Max talking to the control tower at the Red Rock airport and stared out at the ground below, seeing the same sights she'd seen so many times as she'd flown there from Atlanta over the past several months, but seeing them now in such a remarkably different way that it was brand-new.

She didn't interrupt his concentration as he settled the plane on the ground in a way she couldn't help but admire, considering how loudly the air was screaming past the windows. It was like he managed to catch a bullet with goose down. Once they'd landed, he taxied around the airport, clearly knowing where he was going and what he was doing even though to her it all just seemed like a maze, marked with strange signs and markings. He returned the plane to the same tie-down where it had been located before, helped her out and walked her back toward Tanner's hangar.

The sun was beginning to lower, painting the horizon in brilliant reds and oranges. The lights around the airport were coming on.

"I need to take care of some paperwork. It's going to take me a while," he told her as they came abreast of the office door. "There's no reason you need to hang around and be bored."

She wanted to argue that nothing about him bored her, not even waiting quietly for him to complete his tasks. But she suddenly felt tongue-tied. Which she knew was ridiculous considering the way they'd spent the afternoon, but knowing still didn't help. So she didn't voice the question clamoring inside her—would they see one another again?—and made herself nod. She held the bunch of daisies up a few inches. They had finally begun to wilt a little, but she couldn't bear to part with them. "Thank you again, Max. For the flowers. For…everything. It was a wonderful day."

"So polite. Must be that finishing school thing." He smiled slightly. Touched her nose. "You're sunburned. Should have warned you to bring sunblock. Don't want anything hurting that smooth skin of yours."

"I'll be fine." Her skin would be, anyway.

She wasn't so sure about the rest of her. "What, um, what day do you take your exam?"

"Thursday."

"And you're not nervous?"

"Ask me on Thursday." His lips tilted. "Brandi claims I'll be fine. I've sailed through all the practice tests. As long as I keep myself focused, I feel prepared."

Focus. She supposed things kept coming back to that particular point for a reason. She was *supposed* to be brilliant at remaining focused. "And after you have your instrument rating? What then?"

"Then I see what the day brings. Keep working for Tanner if I'm lucky. Register for more college classes."

Her brother-in-law had told her just that morning that he was extremely satisfied with the work Max was doing. But Max was already touchy about the fact that she was related to Tanner. Telling Max that Tanner had spoken to her about him wouldn't help, even if what Tanner had said was completely positive. "Why wouldn't you keep working for him?"

Max just gave a grimace. "At this point, I've learned it's dangerous counting on much of anything. Lost a good job a few years ago and it had nothing to do with me personally at all."

She frowned, feeling like something was slipping right through her fingers, and she wasn't even sure what it was, much less how to stop it. "Doesn't all that uncertainty get to you?"

"It's not uncertainty. It's just life. My life, anyway." He shrugged. "Gotta roll with the punches. Clichéd maybe, but still true."

"So you'll take college classes that you may not even really be interested in?" The idea was a little bewildering. "For what purpose?"

"Keep inching toward a business degree. Sooner or later I'll get there, even if I'm fifty by that time."

She studied his face. Saw determination but not much of anything else. Certainly not the sheer confidence or passion that was there when he'd flown them to that little airfield. "That sort of perseverance is admirable. And it's not that I have anything against business degrees—" she had an MBA of her own "—but if flying is what sets you on fire, why not pursue *that?*"

But he still didn't answer. Just tugged at a lock of her hair and gave that wry smile of his. "Think you're the one Tanner should have on his payroll pushing his flight school."

She swallowed her mounting frustration and

let the matter drop. "Well, he doesn't need me when he's got you. I'm just handy for some extra ideas."

"Speaking of which, we've still got to get together about the website and stuff."

"Right." Even though she was perfectly willing and happy to show him everything she could, she still couldn't help wishing that he would talk instead about getting together for entirely personal reasons.

Only it was becoming increasingly evident to her that he was not going to do that.

Maybe what happened between them hadn't mattered as much to him as it had to her. Or maybe that's just what she deserved when she hadn't been completely forthright with him about her intention to become a parent.

She turned slightly toward the parking lot. "Give me a call when you have some time in your schedule."

"Hey." He caught her hand, pulling her back around. "You're not running off that quick."

Just that easily, her heart started flitting crazily around inside her chest. "You wanted to get to your paperwork," she reminded.

"I *have* to get to it," he corrected. His knuckles nudged her chin until she was looking up at him. Only when she was, did he nod. "Better."

He pressed a soft, lingering kiss on her lips. When he lifted his head and stepped back, she felt positively weak-kneed. "Be careful driving back to Wendy's."

She nodded wordlessly. She simply didn't know what to make of the man or the feelings he roused in her. She turned again toward the lot where her car was only one of a few still parked there. She wasn't even halfway when her feet started dragging.

She couldn't leave like this.

She had to say something. Anything that would let him know that whatever happened in the future, this day had mattered to her.

She stopped and whirled around. "Max—" But all of the urgency that had bubbled up inside her went flat.

She'd expected to see him still watching her, but her eyes didn't find anything behind her at all except the office door swinging closed.

She exhaled, clutched the daisies to her chest and turned once more toward the car.

She didn't even realize until she was nearly at Wendy's home that there were tears sliding down her cheeks.

Chapter 10

"Well? How was it?"

Emily kept her gaze on the screen of her laptop sitting open on the kitchen table in front of her and continued rapidly typing out her usual Monday morning briefing to her assistant, Samantha, and the rest of her staff back in Atlanta. "How was what?"

Wendy huffed and yanked out one of the kitchen chairs, sitting down across from Emily. She propped MaryAnn's diapered bottom on the table and wriggled her bare little feet. "Auntie Emily is playing dumb," she told the baby. "And Mommy isn't buying it for a second."

Emily finished typing her sentence and looked over the computer at her sister. "I *am* working here."

"Then go do it in an office somewhere if you don't want me interrupting," Wendy returned rapidly. "Otherwise, this is my kitchen and I get to ask whatever questions I want."

Emily sighed, pressed the command to send her lengthy message and closed the laptop. She looked at her sister. "It's getting on your nerves, me staying here like this."

Wendy's brows pulled together. "Now you're really being dumb." She reached across the table, squeezing Emily's hand. "I feel like this is the first time you've ever really recognized me as an adult. And I love having you here."

Emily eyed Wendy. "MaryAnne or not, you and Marcos are still newlyweds."

Wendy smiled slyly. "Believe me. We still manage to act like newlyweds whether you know it or not."

Emily groaned a little. "I don't want to know about your sex life."

"Well, I want to know about yours." Wendy covered MaryAnne's ears and grinned. "You slept with him, didn't you, you slept with Max yesterday."

The house had been empty when Emily

arrived home the evening before; both Marcos and Wendy at Red and MaryAnne being minded by Victoria, one of their cousins who'd also recently transplanted herself to Red Rock. "There wasn't any sleeping involved," Emily murmured.

Wendy crowed, took MaryAnne's little hands in hers and clapped them together. "Yay," she said into her daughter's giggling face. "Yay!"

"I seriously think you need to remember what's appropriate content where your daughter is concerned," Emily deadpanned.

Wendy just smiled more widely than ever. "Teaching MaryAnne to cheer," she assured. "So she'll know what to do when Marcos takes her to her first ball game. Isn't that right, my beautiful girl?" She clapped MaryAnne's hands together and the baby chortled and kicked her legs wildly.

Emily watched them, the ache inside her a physical thing. "How soon can you take a home pregnancy test?"

Wendy's eyebrows skyrocketed as she quickly looked at Emily. "I think a day or two after your first missed period. At the earliest. As I recall, a week is the preferred wait. Why are you asking? Dr. Grace is going to test you in a few weeks anyway, isn't she?"

Emily nodded and pushed restlessly away from the table. She went to one of the cupboards and pulled out a coffee mug, only to put it back and pour herself a glass of water, instead. "I just think maybe my hormones are… running amuck. And you did say that when you were pregnant, you were, well, more easily—" She broke off.

Wendy was grinning, clearly relishing Emily's inarticulate moment. She held up one finger. "Horny," she said. "But just hold that thought, would you? I have *got* to call Jordana. She'll never forgive me if she's not in on this."

"Wendy!"

But her sister was already carrying Mary-Anne out of the kitchen, obviously set on her mission.

She wished she'd never opened her mouth and wondered how on earth she could work herself out of it.

The short answer was, she couldn't.

Barely ten minutes later, she was facing down *both* of her younger sisters. And Jordana, whose six-months-pregnant stomach was testing the limits of the sleeveless yellow T-shirt she was wearing, sweet, shy Jordana, was even more merciless than Wendy had been.

"You think the only reason you had such a spectacular—" she glanced at MaryAnne, who was now sitting happily in her playpen waving a plastic block around her head "—*time* with Max, is because you might be pregnant?"

Emily crossed her arms, her chin lifting defensively. "Well, couldn't it? I've never, I mean *never* felt like that with anyone else."

Wendy covered her eyes, muffling her laughter and leaning back in her chair so far that Emily thought she might tip over. Of course, Emily could always push the chair leg and make her tip over. The thought was more than a little tempting.

Jordana was laughing a little, too, though her gaze was a whole lot more sympathetic. "Do you ever consider that it might be the *man* himself you were reacting to? Maybe you really like Max more than you want to admit."

"Of course I like Max! He's intelligent and funny and doesn't give himself nearly as much credit as he should." Emily paced the length of the kitchen cabinets, handed MaryAnne the block she'd tossed out of her playpen, and paced back again. She plopped down on her chair. "If I hadn't liked him I wouldn't have… you know."

"She wasn't wearing a bra under her blouse," Wendy told Jordana as if Emily weren't sitting right there. "She was still wearing her robe and pj's when you and Tanner were here for breakfast. But when she left the house to meet him, she was wearing that white peasant number of mine that I bought a few years ago in Milan."

"Ah." Jordana's gaze slid back to Emily. "So…you went flying with Max already thinking it might lead to a close-up visit with the horizontal."

"I did not," she denied, completely without a speck of truth, whatsoever. "I just borrowed the blouse from Wendy because she has some prettier things than I do."

"Sexier things," Wendy corrected.

Jordana nodded, plucking at her own simple maternity top. "Well, that's true enough. She always paid more attention to her wardrobe than we did."

"I just didn't want to look like I was going to a business meeting at FortuneSouth," Emily muttered.

"Well, you succeeded," Wendy assured humorously.

Emily gestured at Wendy. "And if you'd

have had a strapless bra that would have fit without me having to use a few boxes of tissue as stuffing, I would have worn one!"

"Anyway," Jordana interrupted, "as I was saying, maybe you *really* like Max more than you want to admit."

"And I've already admitted I liked him," Emily said impatiently.

"What Jordana's trying to tactfully suggest is that you might be falling in love with Max," Wendy said bluntly. "Which, frankly, I could have told you days ago."

Emily's chair scooted back with a screech as she shot to her feet. "That's ridiculous."

She saw the look her sisters exchanged.

"Is it?" Jordana asked quietly. "Emily, in all of my life, I've never seen you so worked up over anything. Not even getting our father to recognize that you were more than capable of heading up the advertising department at FortuneSouth."

"Worked up." Emily latched on to the phrase. It not only described the way Max made her feel, it would explain her crying the whole drive home from the airport, even though she'd had nothing to cry about. "That's it exactly. That could be pregnancy hormones. Right?"

Jordana's lips parted. She was eying Emily as if she'd lost her mind.

"For heaven's sake, Emily," Wendy exclaimed. "Would you just look beyond this mommy project of yours for a few minutes?"

Emily's chest felt tight. "But all I want is a baby!"

"That doesn't mean you can't have more," Jordana pointed out gently.

"With Max?" Emily laughed, and even to her own ears it sounded a little wild. "I can't even tell him about my plans because he'd bolt. He still hasn't gotten over giving up Anthony." She pointed at Jordana. "And he doesn't even think he should see me at all because *you're* married to his boss."

"Obviously he doesn't think it really hard, considering he's taken you out several times."

"Not several times," Emily argued.

"Red." Wendy immediately took up Jordana's point and held up her hand, ticking off her fingers.

"That was business."

"You danced," her youngest sister fired back. "That ain't business, honey child." She ticked off a second finger. "Etienne's." She ticked off a third. "Pizza at his place."

"That was the same night as Etienne's," Emily reminded.

"Two meals," Jordana said quickly. "I'd say that counts as two dates."

"Particularly when she didn't come in until after midnight," Wendy added. "Plus, she was wearing his clothes! And then flying yesterday." She held up her four fingers and waved them triumphantly over her head, much the same way that MaryAnne was waving her plastic blocks. "It would take most people six months before they'd spent as much time together as you and Max have."

"And that's not adding in the hours you've spent with him at the flight school," Jordana added.

"For business," Emily reminded doggedly.

"Yeah, but Tanner's commented a few times about how cozy the two of you have looked, hunched together over Max's computer in that cramped office of his."

"He's the one who wanted me to meet with Max!"

"And we all know he never expected you to put in more than a few hours with him. Instead, you've spent *days* with him."

Emily could feel her molars clenching together. "Just because the two of you are head over heels gaga for your husbands does not mean that I am head over heels for Max."

"Who in your entire life have you dated more than twice?" Jordana asked, starting to look a little impatient herself.

Emily pressed her lips together. Because the truth was, besides Max, she'd never dated anyone more than twice, including the other two men she'd slept with. And considering her particularly explosive experiences with Max, it made her vague recollection of those other men so anemic in comparison they might as well have never existed.

"What good would it do to fall for him?" she asked her sisters. "He's never going to let himself fall for me!"

"Ah, honey." Jordana got up and pretty much waddled around the table. She cupped Emily's cheek. "Why on earth wouldn't he?"

Emily stared at Jordana. "I just want to know if I'm pregnant," she complained huskily. "That's all I want to know." She was afraid that was all she could deal with right now.

"But you're just going to have to wait!" Wendy got up from the table, too, and came around to stand next to Emily. "So in the meantime, couldn't you please at least entertain the idea that the connection you feel to Max has everything to do with him, and nothing to do with that vial of Ivy League, Mensa-quality sperm you picked out? What you're feeling could be caused by emotion," Wendy pointed out, as if she were talking to a child, "and not pregnancy hormones."

Emily stared back at her sisters and slowly shook her head. "I don't know," she admitted with painful honesty. "My mommy project, as you call it, is something I can control. If step one doesn't work, I move on to step two. And three and four and five." She had every option already outlined, right down to having the paperwork for foreign adoptions all ready to be filed, if she exhausted every possibility of conceiving, herself.

"Emily," Jordana said, "your single-minded ability to pursue something is as scary as it is impressive. But love doesn't work that way. And maybe, just maybe, the reason why you're feeling so panicked about Max is that somewhere in that overachieving mind of yours, you're realizing that fact yourself. You can't put your heart in a spreadsheet, honey. You can't sit down and outline steps one and two through five or five hundred to help you negotiate your way through loving someone." She lifted her shoulders, her brown eyes steady and filled with an abiding confidence that had only been there since she and Tanner had fallen in love. "For that, you're just going to have to put your heart out there."

Emily felt a burning deep behind her eyes. "And if I end up the only one with my heart dangling in the breeze?"

"That's a chance we all take."

She looked at her two sisters. Live-wire, creative Wendy, who was the perfect complement to Marcos's Latino passion. And gentle, brilliant Jordana, who was clearly yin to Tanner's former military yang.

Could she ever be that sort of perfect fit for Max, and he for her?

The thought was more terrifying than she wanted to admit.

Not because she didn't want it.

But because, no matter what she told her sisters, she was starting to suspect that she did.

"How am I going to get through the next few weeks until I can take that test?"

Wendy shook her head slightly. Shared a frustrated look with Jordana. "While there are times when I really envy your ability to focus on the future, I can tell you that you need to stop looking so hard at what's up ahead and start enjoying what's going on in the here and now."

"See what the day brings?" Emily murmured. Max's words.

Wendy and Jordana both looked surprised. Then relieved. As if Emily had finally grasped some of their point.

"Exactly."

The *day* didn't bring Max. Nor did the next.

Emily did everything she could think of to fill her days. To do that whole "live for the moment" thing and stop worrying about what she couldn't control. She took MaryAnne for walks in her stroller, found a pretty park and held her on her lap as she sat in one of the swings, swaying back and forth. She called a Realtor and visited several condominiums, and even a pretty house on a hill that was near Max's neighborhood and already possessed a wonderful little nursery. She dealt with matters at the office, and sat in on conference calls, made notes and decisions. She called her mother and listened to Virginia Alice's lilting voice as she described every detail of a garden party she was throwing for one of the charities she supported. She even tried her hand at making a batch of pastries with Wendy in the kitchen at Red while the rest of the restaurant was still and quiet.

Nothing, not one single thing, not for one single moment, was enough to keep her mind off Max.

So when Wednesday came and went, with still no word from Max, and her father called late in the afternoon asking her to fly back to Atlanta because the Connover deal had hit a snag, she couldn't find a single reason not to. She caught a red-eye and was in the FortuneSouth offices bright and early Thursday morning.

But even there, while she sat around the conference table and did her part in reiterating to the Connover folks all the reasons why FortuneSouth was the answer to their woes, she couldn't forget that Max was taking his instrument exam that day. And when they stopped the meeting for a well-needed break, she avoided her father who clearly wanted to talk to her, and closed herself in her office, telling Samantha that she didn't want to be disturbed.

Pride had kept her from calling Max before.

But not now.

She dialed the flight school, and paced around the desk in her office, her heart seeming to knock against the wall of her chest as she waited for an answer. She stared out the windows lining the walls behind her desk, not really seeing anything of the view below because visions of daisies were swimming in her mind.

Then, suddenly, his deep voice was in her ear, and her throat closed up, barely allowing her to get a word out at all. "This is Emily Fortune," she finally managed, and then wanted to fall through a hole to the center of the earth.

"Well, hello there, This-Is-Emily-Fortune," he drawled, obviously amused. "What's up?"

She thumped her hand against her forehead, glad that he was on the other end of a phone line and couldn't see her. "I just wanted to wish you good luck today. You know. With the exam."

She heard a faint squeak in the background and all too easily envisioned him sitting at his desk in his usual chair. "Thanks."

Emily switched her cell phone from one nervously damp hand to her other and cleared her throat. "Listen, Max, I—"

"Emily, I've—" he said at the same time.

They both stopped.

He made a sound that could have been anything from a cough to a laugh. "You first," he said.

She swallowed. "I... I didn't really call to wish you luck. I mean, I did. I *do*. Wish you luck, that is. Not that you'll need it." Dear Lord. She was supposed to possess some ability when it came to words. "I just wanted to tell you that I... I really enjoyed spending last Sunday with you." She couldn't hear anything on his end of the line. Not even the faint squeak of his desk chair. She closed her eyes tightly. "It meant a lot to me," she finally finished.

"And you're probably wondering why I haven't called you since," he said after a moment.

She pinched the bridge of her nose. Hanging in the breeze, indeed. "Not at all," she lied. "I know you're a busy man."

"Always that positive spin on things, eh, Emily Fortune?"

Her knees felt shaky. She sat down on the edge of her desk and stared at her pale reflection in the decorative mirror on the wall across from her. She had circles under her eyes. Probably from too many sleep-interrupted nights jerking wide awake to the realization he'd only been making love to her in her dreams. "Okay," she said huskily. "Why haven't you?"

"Because you make it way too easy for me to forget everything else." She heard him exhale. "And it has been a crazy few days. I've been cramming for the exam every night after work with Brandi and Ross. Guess I'm more worried about it than I expected."

"Oh, Max," she murmured. "You're going to do brilliantly. I know you will."

He gave a half laugh that didn't sound particularly amused. "I wanted to call. Nearly did about a few dozen times."

"Gotta get a buzz going on the internet any way we can about Redmond Flight School?"

"That's one reason," he allowed. "Only Tanner's been dealing with all the FAA requirements we've still got to meet in order to hit the launch for Redmond Charter in a few weeks, so he's got me handling the reservations that're already coming in as well as all the other scheduling. That's kind of put kick-starting the social media thing for a bunch of high school kids on the back burner."

"Well, that's understandable. Business obviously isn't faltering as a result."

"No. But Tanner's got his plans and he hasn't forgotten about the website or anything. He doesn't do anything halfway."

She looked away from her reflection. Tanner wasn't the only one with that particular trait.

"He's also decided to hire a receptionist," Max was saying. "I talked to him about the advantage of having her—or him—have the skills to update the website, keep all that on-line stuff going once we get it started."

"That sounds good," she said faintly.

"Right. He agreed. But I just placed the ad yesterday afternoon and had over four hundred resumes in my email this morning."

"So you've been slammed."

"I still should have called." He was silent for a moment. "It meant something to me, too, Emily. A lot, if we're being truthful here, and maybe I'm not adjusting to that fact as well as I should."

She let out a miserable laugh. "That sounds painfully familiar, actually."

"It does?"

She had to deliberately lighten her hold on the phone because her fingers were cramping. "I told you personal relationships weren't my forte, remember?"

"I figured you were being hard on yourself."

"Oh, Max." She looked upward and shook her head. "Maybe you and I are more alike than we thought."

"I don't know, This-Is-Emily-Fortune. That's a pretty hard one to wrap my mind around."

Despite everything, she felt her lips twitch. "You're going to rib me about that from now on, I suppose."

"Hell, yes," he said immediately. "Otherwise I'll keep forgetting that you're not perfect."

"If I were perfect I wouldn't feel knotted up inside when it comes to you."

"Good knots or bad knots?"

"Good." She hoped. "Listen." She straightened her spine. The break was only supposed to be for ten minutes, and she didn't want her father coming to look for her. She ran her palms down the thighs of her slacks. "You're right. Don't worry about the website or anything. That's absolutely not a priority for you right now. Just focus on that exam and go into it with a positive attitude."

"Yes, ma'am." He sounded amused. "Anything else?"

"A little bossy, I guess."

"In the nicest of ways."

"Now, *you're* just being finishing school polite."

He laughed softly. "Baby, the only thing finishing school and I have in common is *you*."

Baby. He'd called her that when they'd made love. When she'd felt like her world was spinning out of control. Her gaze fastened on her reflection again, needing to see that she was still in her suit with her hair tied back, and not wearing a peasant blouse with a daisy tucked behind her ear.

She heard a soft knocking, and looked over to see her assistant waving at her from behind the glass door. Samantha exaggeratedly pointed at her watch.

Emily nodded and looked down at the toes of her black pumps. "Maybe you're right about that particular point," she said into the phone, "but I think I'm right that we might both be too hard on ourselves. And as good as it is to hear your voice, I've got a meeting to get back to."

"In Red Rock?"

She shook her head even though he couldn't see it. "I'm in my office in Atlanta, actually."

"Corner office, I'll bet."

She couldn't deny it. "I had to come back to take care of some things."

"When're you coming home?"

She closed her eyes for a moment, something sweet flowing through her. Home. Did he really think of Red Rock as her home, too?

"As soon as I can." The words were almost a whisper. "It might be early next week."

"Call me," he said. Then his voice dropped a notch. "I'll pick you up from the airport."

Samantha tapped on the glass door again. Emily didn't even glance at her. "That sounds really good," she told him. "Will you, um, will you call me tonight? After you're done with your exam? Tell me how it went?"

"It might be late. You're an hour ahead of me."

"It doesn't matter how late," she assured.

"Maybe I should call really late. Make sure you're alone. In bed. Give me a chance to imagine what you're wearing."

She swallowed. Swift heat streaked through her.

But her office door opened, and her father stood there, looking impatient. Behind him, Samantha gave Emily an apologetic shrug.

Emily moistened her lips and straightened off the desk. "That definitely sounds like an interesting conversation," she said crisply.

Max laughed softly and it was all she could do not to shiver with delight. "Someone's there, I take it."

"Exactly."

"So what would you say if I told you that you have the sweetest tasting nipples I've ever kissed? And your—"

She whirled around to face the windows, her eyes feeling like they wanted to roll back in her head. "That's a hard one to figure," she interrupted. "I'm afraid I'll need more time than I have at the moment."

He laughed. "Hard is right. Have a good meeting, Emily Fortune. Think of me."

The line went dead and she closed her eyes, counting to ten. The problem was nearly all she could do was think of Max.

"Emily," John Michael said from behind her. "If you can *possibly* fit us back into your schedule?"

She slid her phone back into her pocket and whirled around to face her father with the same bright, confident smile she'd perfected in her bathroom mirror when she'd been only eighteen and he'd warned her that if she messed up as an intern at FortuneSouth, she'd be fired just like anyone else. "Sorry, Dad. It was just something that I needed to take care of back in Red Rock." She marched past him out the office door.

"Maybe you ought to be taking care of

things that matter *here,*" he said impatiently, easily keeping pace with her. "You have responsibilities here, Emily. If you aren't willing to make them your priority, then I'll find someone else who will."

She stopped in her tracks right there in the middle of the corridor, feeling something inside her snapping into place. She looked up at him. "Frankly, Daddy, I'm not interested in these threats of yours. At this point, I've just heard too many." For the first time in her career, she didn't even care that employees were coming and going all around them and any one of them could overhear. "If you're going to fire me, then do it and get it over with."

At sixty-two, John Michael Fortune still cut an intimidating figure. Well over six feet, with a thick head of salt-and-pepper hair, she'd known more than one employee who'd practically crawled away after earning one of his famous, disapproving looks.

She certainly was earning one of his looks at that very moment. Could see the steam gathering in his thunderous expression.

And if she'd wondered what the answer would be if her position at FortuneSouth came down to the wire, she realized that she knew the answer now.

She lifted her chin a little. "Otherwise, get off my back and let me do my job. If you can't do that, then I'll just write up my own resignation letter and neither one of us will have to worry about pleasing each other again."

"Emily!" He'd gone from looking thunderous to shocked in the span of a heartbeat. "What on earth would you do without FortuneSouth? This is your life here!"

She stared at him. FortuneSouth was *not* her life. Not anymore.

She looked around him and spotted Samantha, watching openmouthed from her office door. "Type up a standard resignation letter for my father," she said clearly. "Tell him I'll give two weeks' notice and not one day more. I'll sign the letter after I'm through with this meeting."

And then she turned around and headed back to the conference room and the people waiting there.

It was almost as big a rush as it had been taking off in that little plane with Max.

Chapter 11

"You did what?" Emily's mother, Virginia Alice, stared at Emily with horror. Emily had two suitcases thrown open on top of her bed, and was neatly and rapidly filling them with the clothes from her closet.

Trousers. Blouses. Dresses.

Everything but suits.

She'd had enough of those to last a lifetime.

She eyed the tailored shirt in her hand and tossed it aside, reaching instead for an emerald sundress that was easily ten years old, but at least didn't look like it belonged in a corporate office. "I resigned," she told her mom patiently. "Gave Dad a letter offering two weeks' notice and he tossed it back in my face. Told me if I was going to go, I might as well do it now." She fit the dress into the suitcase. "Despite the fact that I've been able to handle my job at FortuneSouth just fine since I've been going to Red Rock, he's obviously not satisfied with any commitments I make there. He wants me gone and believe me, I'm happy to go."

"What commitments?" Her mother shook her perfectly styled silver-haired head. She was dressed as impeccably as ever in a pale pink crushed-silk pants suit, but she looked positively bewildered and had from the moment she'd appeared at Emily's apartment door. "You mean this plan of yours to have a baby?"

"That." Emily turned back to her closet. "And…anything else I might be involved with."

"Ah. Shouldn't that be any*one* else?"

Emily turned and looked at her mother. Speculation had replaced bewilderment.

"I do talk to Jordana and Wendy nearly every day," Virginia Alice pointed out. "Just because you haven't told me anything about this Max Allen you've been seeing doesn't mean they haven't."

Thoroughly nonplussed, Emily sat down on the bed. It was six o'clock in the evening. Max was probably already undergoing his exam now, and Emily's mother should have been at home, pouring John Michael's pre-dinner drink just like she'd been doing for years and years and years. "I…didn't know what to tell you," she finally admitted.

Virginia Alice sat on the bed on the other side of the suitcases and crossed her legs. "Wendy thinks you're in love with him. Why don't we start there. *Are* you?"

Emily opened her mouth, the automatic denial at the ready. Then she lifted her shoulders instead. "How can I be? I've only known him a few weeks!"

Virginia Alice smiled slightly. "I knew I was going to marry your father the night I met him." Her gaze went toward the industrial-height ceiling of Emily's loft and she shook her head. "Fell head over heels in love with him the moment he smiled at me and said my name for the first time. Oh, he had such ambition. All he could talk about was starting his own business. Changing the world with it." Her lips curved. "All *I* could think about was how ridiculously handsome he was and how soon I could maneuver him into kissing me while letting him think it was all his own idea. That's the thing about your daddy, you know. As long as he thinks he's the one that came up with the idea, a person can get him to agree to most…anything. Why, that man was nearly puritanical until he met me."

Emily stared. "Mom!"

Her mother's cheeks looked a little pink. "Surely you don't think passion only came into existence with your generation?"

"Well, *no,* but I've never heard you say such things."

Virginia Alice folded her hands demurely. "In my day, a lady just didn't say them. But that certainly didn't mean we didn't think or feel or act on such things. We just…tried to keep those matters private."

Emily covered her eyes. She wasn't certain that she didn't wish her mother hadn't continued that particular practice. First it was Wendy and Jordana. Now their genteel, Southern mother?

"And, of course, we had to be smart enough not to get caught with our skirts around our ears and end up having to plan a hurry-up wedding," her mother was adding.

"Mom!"

"Oh, Emily. Stop cringing. You're an adult. Certainly adult enough to go off trying to have a baby on your own, just you and some—" her mother waved her hand "—anonymous man's deposit in one of those *banks*."

Emily groaned. She leaned over until her face was pressed against the cool gray of the quilted cotton coverlet folded over the bottom of her mattress. "You're killing me, Mom," she muttered.

Virginia Alice sighed. "I should have talked about these things more when you and your sisters were younger," she mused. "Been more open about the things that go on between a man and a woman. Maybe you wouldn't be so uptight now."

Emily straightened like a shot. "I'm not uptight."

"*Reserved,* then," her mother appeased. "Now please. I'd like to hear more about this Max since he's clearly the only person you've ever met who matters enough to you that you'll fly in the face of your father."

Emily shrugged, feeling helpless. "He's wonderful. He's smart and hardworking and he *really* loves to fly."

"And how does he feel about this—" Virginia Alice waved her hand again "—baby business?"

"I haven't told him," Emily admitted.

Her mother's eyebrows lifted. "Why ever not?"

"Because things aren't that settled between us," she defended. "And...and I didn't want to scare him off." She pressed her hand against her belly, imaging the tiny being growing inside her at that very moment. "I don't even know if I'm pregnant right this very minute." But she already strongly suspected she was. "That's a hard thing to tell a man you've barely just met!" Particularly one who'd already made it plain he didn't think children were meant to be part of his life.

"Barely just met or not, I can see you're crazy about him, simply by looking into your pretty face. Are you sleeping with him?"

Emily stared, her cheeks turning hot. She felt more like a teenaged girl than a grown woman set on one day having a teenager of her own.

Virginia Alice obviously took Emily's silence as her answer. She tsked. "Nothing good is ever going to come out of keeping a secret like this from someone you love." She leaned over the suitcases and patted Emily's cheek as if she were still no older than a child. "You go on back and you tell this man the truth. Tell him how badly you want a baby in your arms. A baby you can call your own. If he's your perfect match, believe me, it will all turn out just fine."

"We're too different to be a perfect match." If she said the words often enough, maybe she'd feel more convinced.

Virginia Alice just tsked again. "Your daddy and I are pretty darn different, but I think we've made a pretty darn perfect pair. Doesn't mean it's been a walk in the park, now. Your father isn't always the easiest of men, but then again, I'm not always the easiest of women."

"You're a saint compared to daddy."

Virginia Alice waved her hand, dismissing the very notion without needing to say a single word about it. "Being different isn't necessarily a bad thing if those differences complement each other." She lowered her hand and pushed to her feet, brushing her hands down the front of her slacks. "You go do what you need to do. And in the meantime, I'll work on your daddy. We're just not going to let him lose the best advertising director there is because he's too stubborn to see past that darned handsome nose on his face."

Emily stood, too, smiling a little as she shook her head. "Mom. I've resigned. And I feel fine about it. Truly, I do." She wasn't sure what she was going to do exactly, but she'd figure it out. "Maybe I'll try to start up my own advertising firm."

Virginia Alice sniffed a little. "Well, *I* don't feel fine about it. You're more than capable of starting up anything you want, but John pushed you to this point and frankly, he needs to get with the times."

Emily nearly choked. Get with the times? "I'm not sure I recognize you right now."

"Well," Virginia Alice murmured, "seems as if half my family is moving to Texas these days, so I guess it's time I got with the times, too. Sometimes I think he might as well open a FortuneSouth office in Red Rock. The only one he's got left here who matters to him now is your brother Michael, and at the rate John's going, who knows how long it'll be before he drives him off, too! And then there will be nobody left to take over the reins for him. One of these days I expect to have him to myself again, and not be sharing him with Fortune-South every minute of the day. Someone has to do something, and it might as well be me." She smiled the same gentle smile she'd always had. "It might shock you, Emily dear, but even at my age, I still have my ways."

* * *

"I passed."

Emily clutched the phone tightly at the sound of Max's voice. It was almost midnight and she'd begun to think he wasn't going to call after all. She rested her head against the pillows mounded behind her and turned off the rerun of the evening news she'd been watching, plunging her bedroom into darkness. "I knew you would pass."

"Yeah. Well. Positive thinking doesn't always turn out positively. Where are you?"

She smiled slightly and plucked at the coverlet covering her knees. "Home. Where are you?"

"Home. Had dinner over at Kirsten and Jeremy's. She insisted on celebrating."

"I'm glad she did. You *should* celebrate. And we'll celebrate again when I see you." In fact, she felt giddy anticipation leaping around inside her knowing how soon that would be.

"Where are you at home?"

Her gaze drifted over the lofty shadows of her high ceilings. "In my bedroom." She was glad there was no one there to see the silly smile on her face. "You?"

"Sitting on one of the bar stools in my dining room and remembering you in my kitchen two feet from where I'm sitting now, wearing practically nothing more than one of my shirts," he continued.

She was wearing the Rangers T-shirt at that very moment and at his words, her skin went just as hot and prickly as it had that night with him.

"How'd the meeting go?"

She nearly had to kick-start her brain. "Interesting," she finally said. She didn't want to tell him about quitting her job on the phone. "I'll tell you about it when I get back tomorrow."

"Must've gone well if you're coming back that soon. You taking a charter?"

"Commercial actually." Now that she wouldn't be traveling on FortuneSouth business, she had no excuse to use the charter service. "I'll be flying into San Antonio. Getting in around eight tomorrow evening." It had been the earliest seat she could find.

"I'll pick you up."

"You don't have to go to that trouble." It would have been different if her flight had gone directly to Red Rock.

"Driving twenty miles to San Antonio isn't exactly trouble." He waited a beat. "We can go out to dinner if you're interested."

Interested didn't come close. "As long as it's not Etienne's."

He laughed. "Not Etienne's," he agreed. "Maybe…stay overnight there. Celebrate a little more."

Desire cramped through her. "Okay. I, um, I have something I wanted to talk to you about, too."

"I've got some news, myself," he said. "Tomorrow's soon enough for that. Right now I just want to know what you're wearing. And if you say nothing, I'm not going to believe you, because I'm pretty sure This-Is-Emily-Fortune has never slept in the buff in her life."

She sank a few inches lower against the pillows. Max *did* know her. "I'm wearing the shirt you loaned me," she admitted huskily.

"Anything else?"

"Underwear."

"Panties," he corrected. "That's the word if you wanna get a man thinking, baby."

"Fine. *Panties*." She pushed out the word. And even though she was alone and there was a thousand miles between them, his soft chuckle told her he knew exactly how hard she was blushing. "You might be familiar with them," she added, determined to share the torture. "They have a tiny white bow right over my—"

"Okay, okay," he cut her off. "I get the picture."

She smiled into the darkness which was alleviated only by the moonlight shining through the unadorned windows near the ceiling. For the first time, she realized the windows were very similar to the windows in the flight school hangar.

"You can text me your flight info and I'll be waiting," he said after moment. It wasn't quite what she'd expected him to say.

She slid even lower against the pillows. Wondering if he could hear the rustle of her movements over the phone line. "Don't you want to know anything else?" she asked, and was thrilled with the way her voice came out all throaty and wholly *un*-Emily-like.

"I've created a monster."

"Are you hard, Max?" she whispered. "Because I am so, so—"

He muttered an oath. "Stop. There's not gonna be enough cold water in Texas to cool me down."

She laughed softly. Considering everything, maybe she had a little more of the surprising woman that Virginia Alice Fortune was turning out to be in her than she'd thought. "Sweet dreams, Max."

"Wait until tomorrow, Emily, and I'll give you sweet."

She laughed again and ended the call, then set the phone on her nightstand and turned over, hugging the pillow to her cheek.

And thinking of Max, and only Max, she went blissfully to sleep.

Waiting for Emily's plane to land the next evening was about the biggest exercise in patience that Max had ever endured.

It was late.

Not just a few minutes late. Seventy-two minutes late. He kept abreast of the flight details online and left Red Rock when the jetliner was an hour out. But even then, he had to cool his heels, pacing around the terminal area until the status board indicated that her plane had landed. Then, even though it had, it just seemed to mean more waiting.

He raked his hand through his hair and stared at the end of the gate area where he knew she'd have to pass through.

"Waiting for someone special?"

The voice came out of nowhere, and he looked to his side at the wizened old man who was sitting nearby in a motorized chair. "Yeah. You?"

The old guy smiled and nodded, tapping his hand against the armrest of his chair. "M'daughter and her kids. Boy and a girl. Twelve-year-old twins. Coming to spend a few weeks with me." He shook his head, but he was obviously pleased. "Don't know if my house'll still be standin' by the time they're done." He gave a wheezy sort of laugh.

"Sounds like a good way to celebrate to me," Max offered, his gaze straying back toward the gates.

"Yeah, it is," the man agreed. "Wish m' wife were still here to share it, but wasn't meant to be." He sighed a little.

Max looked back at the guy. "How long were you married?"

"Damn near sixty years," he said. "I'm ninety-two. If I'd been smarter when I was a pup like you, I'd a' married her sooner and we'd a' had longer together." The old man suddenly pointed, his wrinkled face crinkling into a wide grin. "There they are now."

Max looked over toward the gates. But it wasn't the teenaged kids jogging out of the gate who looked like carbon copies of each other or the harried woman chasing after them and waving toward the old man that held his attention. It was Emily who was not far behind them who did that.

No ponytail.

No suit.

Just a close-fitting knee-length yellow dress that buttoned all the way down the front, and two suitcases that she was dragging behind her.

Leaving the old man to his family reunion, Max strode forward and met Emily. "I didn't get any sleep last night," he greeted.

She stopped a few feet shy of him, her eyes sparkling behind her glasses. "That's so strange," she commented with a demure smile. "I slept like a baby."

"Sure you did." He slowly advanced on her, loving the fact that she merely lifted that perfectly pointed chin of hers and held her ground, even though her peridot gaze was dancing shyly away from his. "Talking the way you were, getting a guy all worked up only to leave him hanging in the breeze—" He slid his arm around her shoulders and pulled her up onto her toes to press a brief kiss on her lips. "Naturally you slept like a baby."

She let out a blushing laugh as she looked up at him. "You were the one who started it, telling me what you did on the phone when you knew I had people around me in my office."

"Bothered you, did it?"

She pressed her lips together, probably trying to look prim and not managing it at all.

He laughed, kissed her again and set her from him to take over the suitcases. He wasn't sure he remembered ever having a reason to laugh as often as he had since he'd met her.

"Do you have more luggage or is this it?" She had her briefcase hanging from her shoulder and was carrying another smaller tote bag as well. He was a little surprised by the load, considering how light she'd traveled the other time she'd gone to Atlanta.

"This is it." For a second she looked like she was going to say more, but all she did was hitch the strap on her shoulder a little higher, and they fell into step.

Max's gaze met the old guy's as they passed him and his family, and the man nodded toward Emily, giving a thumbs-up. Max grinned and would've given him one back if his hands hadn't been full carrying her suitcases.

Emily noticed, giving him a curious look as they headed toward the nearest exit. "What was that all about?"

"Just a guy thing." He slowed his steps so he didn't outpace her. "How was the flight?"

"Bumpy. Late." They'd quickly reached the exit and she preceded him out the door into the night air. She glanced over her shoulder at him. "I warned you this would be too much trouble. It's not like being able to just step outside your office at the flight school and, voilà, there's the terminal."

"And I told you it was fine." He stopped at the curb and lowered the suitcases to the cement, then scooped his arm around her waist, pulling her in for another kiss. This one managing to leave his control feeling a little shredded because of the way her tongue boldly snuck up against his. He lifted his head. "We're in public here," he reminded gruffly.

"Is that a complaint?"

He brushed his mouth against her ear. "Only because you're making me even more impatient to get you alone. And I planned to take you to dinner. Remember?"

She twisted her head around, looking up at him. Despite the artificial light illuminating the area, everything about her seemed to glow from some inner source. Behind her glasses, her eyes were bright. "And after you've fed me?"

"I found us a room at a B and B down by

the River Walk." Where he fully intended to feast on her.

"A B and B?" She looked delighted. "How charming."

"Here's hoping. I took the only room that I found available on such short notice," he warned. "I'm not sure what room we'll end up with there since their website wasn't particularly clear." The B and B obviously didn't have a person like Emily to help with such matters. "Otherwise it would have been just a regular old hotel room or my bed back at my place."

She watched him. "Your place would have been fine with me," she said softly.

Maybe it would have been. But she just seemed to deserve something more out of the ordinary for her first night back. And at least he'd done more investigating about the B and B than he had Etienne's. "Consider it part of the celebrating," he said. She didn't even know yet the other reason he had for celebration.

"Well." She made a little production of removing her glasses and tucking them away inside her purse before looking up at him again. "If it's all the same to you, can we just head on to the B and B? I'm pretty tired. It's been a busy day."

He frowned, a little concerned. She'd always

seemed to have the stamina of five strapping men, all packed up in one svelte, cool-looking blonde. But she did have shadows under her eyes when he looked closely. "Sure. You can take a bath. Relax. Head straight to bed if you want."

"Max?" She looped her finger in the V of his polo shirt and tugged his head toward her. "What I want is you," she said softly, but distinctly. "So can we go straight to the B and B?"

His mouth dried. He eyed the color rising in her cheeks, the glow of her eyes. "Yeah," he managed. "Straight there."

She smiled slowly. Slid her finger free and turned toward the parking lot across the roadway. "Please tell me you're parked close."

Thankfully, he was.

When they reached his truck, he unlocked the door and helped her up on the high seat, not bothering to pretend he wasn't admiring the length of her smooth legs below the knee-length dress. Then he stowed her suitcases in the back and drove out of the airport lot with rigid circumspection considering how he felt like racing to the B and B.

Once they did arrive, she told him she had everything she needed in her tote bag so he locked her suitcases and briefcase inside the truck cab and they went inside with just her tote bag and his.

The second they went inside the large Victorian, Emily immediately headed across the foyer area to the opened French doors that led off the rear of the building. Outside, they could hear music and see a small crowd of people.

"Wedding," the girl who greeted them said. "We have a lot of them here." She handed over a large key to Max when he signed his name on the form. "But you don't have to worry about any noise, Mr. Allen. You're in the private cottage across the lawn." She gestured toward another French door, this one opening off to the side of the property. "I'm afraid there's not any parking available closer to the cottage, but you can walk from here."

He didn't care about parking. He did care about privacy. "Thanks." He pocketed the key and went over to retrieve Emily, sliding his arm around her waist because he couldn't stop himself.

She leaned back against his shoulder, glancing up at him. "Look at them," she said softly, obviously meaning the bride and groom laughing together out on the fenced patio that overlooked the river. "They look so happy, they ought to be on the cover of a magazine."

The couple did look happy. "Wonder if they'll still look as happy in a few years when life turns out not to be as pretty as a perfect wedding day."

She slid him a look. "Don't you think their lives might just get better together as they go along?"

He shrugged. "If they beat the odds." And then, because there was a little frown tugging her smooth eyebrows together, he wished he'd just kept his comments to himself. He flattened his palm over her stomach, lowering his mouth to kiss her right below her ear. "Wanna hear my other news?"

As he'd hoped, the move erased the little frown. Her hand slid over his, moving back and forth a little restlessly. "Yes."

"Tanner called me into his office yesterday morning," he began. His boss had looked so damn serious that Max had thought he'd done something wrong. "He said he'd been relying on me more than he'd expected, and that he'd been thinking about his staffing problems for a while and that he needed a manager." Max still could hardly believe what had followed. "I told him that I'd put up an ad, same as I did for the receptionist spot, but he just shook his head and said it wasn't necessary. That the spot was already mine. If I wanted."

"Max! That's wonderful." The true, surprised pleasure on Emily's face told him that she really *hadn't* known. He'd even bluntly asked Tanner if the fact that he'd been seeing Emily had had anything to do with the promotion, and Tanner had denied it. But until that moment, Max realized he'd still harbored a few doubts that she might know more about his career at Redmond Flight School than he did.

He cleared his throat, feeling a little like some kid blowing his own horn to impress a pretty girl. She still didn't know the most important part. The thing that had meant the most. "Anyway, he said I could either take the raise the job comes with, or I could work on my commercial license in trade, instead."

"And once you have that, could you be one of his charter pilots?" she asked, looking excited. "He talked to you about it, didn't he? I can tell by looking at your face that he did."

He and Tanner had talked a long time about Max's options. Long enough that it was finally sinking in that Max wouldn't be going anywhere. Not unless he chose to. And when Max had asked Tanner outright why he was putting so much faith in him, Tanner had just looked right back at him, steady as the day is long. "Why wouldn't I? I think this place means almost as much to you as it does to me. And I need somebody I can count on. You're that somebody."

Now, Max looked at Emily and didn't think about the fact that she was his boss's sister-in-law. He thought about the fact that she was his woman. For however long it lasted. "Some day, yeah, it's possible that I could be flying for Redmond Charter. If it's what I decide I still want." He lowered his mouth close to her ear again. "But what I want right now is to get to our room."

He felt the breath she inhaled. Then she took his hand and followed him out the other door. They crossed the summer-sweet grass to the cottage, which looked pretty much like a miniature version of the main building. Max unlocked the door and they went inside. Emily dropped her purse on the floor, and he dumped the totes alongside it.

He wasn't sure if he reached for her or if she turned into his arms first, but it didn't really matter. Because she was finally there, her mouth opening under his, her fingers tangling in his hair.

One part of him realized he hadn't shut the

cottage door and he backed her up against it until he heard it latch, and his hand swiped over it until he found the lock and turned it. And then because it struck him that the door was a remarkably convenient surface, he stayed there, leaning into her, feeling her arms, her legs, everything about her opening, welcoming him.

He managed to hit a light switch on the wall by the door, and lifting her right off the ground, he turned and carried her across the room to the high, brass bed that the soft light had revealed. Before he even settled her in the center of the bed she was pulling at his belt, dropping little kisses down the center of his chest that burned right through the shirt he was still wearing.

He groaned and pressed her back against the bed, tore the shirt over his head and returned to her, flicking open every single button of the butter-yellow dress until he could spread it wide, feeling like he was unwrapping the most longed-for gift.

Lacy white cups molded her breasts. Matching lace panties were cut high on her long, lean legs. He wrapped his hand around her waist and rolled her against him.

Her eyes met his. "I missed you," she whispered, "manager Max."

He felt his lips tilt. He'd missed her, too. But a lifetime of knocks wouldn't let the words out and all he could do was thread his fingers through her silky hair, spreading it out around her like a white-gold halo. "And every time I close my eyes, I think of you like this, This-Is-Emily-Fortune."

"Naked on a bed?" She smiled broadly, obviously not particularly offended by the idea.

He drew his finger down her nose, moved it over her soft, perfectly shaped lips. "Looking white and glowing like some sort of angel."

Her smile died and her eyes turned soft. Hazy. She slowly lifted her hands, cupping his face. Then she leaned up and pressed her lips against his, so softly and gently that it made something in his chest ache.

"Did you bring an entire box of the, um, you-know-whats?" she whispered.

It took him a half a beat. Then he laughed softly. His shyly passionate angel. "Close enough."

She slid her arm around his back, pulling him down to her, tangling her long leg around his. "Perfect," she whispered throatily. "You can go get one in just a minute," she promised.

It was a little more than a minute.

And it was more than one that he ended up getting.

But long after they were both finally, totally spent and Emily was sprawled against him, taking up her share of the bed as well as his, Max lay there staring into the shadows.

It did feel perfect.

But he knew from experience that things far less perfect hadn't lasted.

So how could this?

Chapter 12

They had breakfast on the small, private terrace that the cottage possessed, overlooking the River Walk while it was still so early that the only people around were an occasional jogger and someone walking their dog. After showering together—another first that not only had them running out of hot water but had Emily corralling the flood of water that escaped with the thick, terry cloth robes the B and B thoughtfully provided—they went exploring. They walked along the famous urban park themselves as it slowly became more busy with shops opening, artisans setting out their wares. Max even bought her a narrow sterling bracelet with a daisy dangling from it and fastened it right around her wrist.

She'd held it up and jiggled the dangling white daisy, hard-pressed not to cry over the sweet feelings burgeoning inside her. "It's the prettiest thing I've ever received," she'd told him.

He'd just smiled indulgently and flicked his finger against the diamond drop hanging at her throat before sliding his fingers through hers and pulling her off to the next stand.

They'd eaten spicy empanadas that they'd washed down with icy lemonade and since they still had a while before they had to turn in the cottage key, they'd returned to the old-fashioned brass bed where he slipped her out of the red sundress she was wearing and they made love yet again.

It was evening by the time they drove back to Red Rock, and Emily knew that in her wildest dreams she couldn't imagine ever feeling as happy as she did sitting beside Max. Seeing the smile on his face, the light in his eyes that seemed to be there now even when he wasn't flying.

But she still needed to tell him.

And the longer she waited, the harder it was becoming.

Just when she'd start to think she'd garnered the nerve to bring it up, he'd tell her something that made her laugh, or start talking about the flight school and be so engaged in what he was saying that she couldn't bear to stop him, or he'd run his fingers down her spine and cause her to simply be unable to think at all.

Which is how she found herself lying beside him that night, in his very own bed, listening to him snore softly while his arm rested heavy and warm over her hips, with the words to tell him what she'd done still locked away inside her.

Light was streaming through the slats of the wide blinds hanging in Max's bedroom window when he woke the next morning. His arm was asleep from where Emily's head was resting, but he didn't care.

He slowly brushed her hair away from her cheek but she didn't stir. And even though he was strongly tempted to slide his hand beneath the T-shirt of his that she was wearing and find the warmth he knew would be waiting, he let her sleep undisturbed. He carefully worked his arm out from beneath her head before sliding off the bed, and smiled when she sighed and dragged his pillow against her cheek, rolling over right to the spot he'd just vacated, her long legs stretching out.

He smiled. "Bed hog," he murmured.

She slept on.

He quietly grabbed some clean clothes and left the bedroom, pulling the door shut so he wouldn't disturb her. He showered and dressed and went down to retrieve Mrs. Sheckley's newspaper and deliver it to her. By the time he escaped from her a half hour later, returning with a dozen blueberry muffins that were heavy enough to be used as door stops, he could hear the shower running and knew that Emily was awake.

He left the muffins in the kitchen and went to the bathroom door, knocking loud enough that she'd hear over the water. "I can make eggs or I can wash your back. Take your pick," he said through the door. He knew which he preferred, but he was pretty content, either way. He liked the idea of sitting at his counter eating breakfast with her. Maybe afterward, they'd go out to the Double Crown, beg a few horses off of Lily for the afternoon and go horseback riding. "Emily?" He knocked again, louder. "You want some breakfast?"

He heard a muffled sound. Then her voice, that didn't sound like her voice at all. "Fine."

He frowned. Cracked the door open. "What's wrong? Are you sick?"

The shower stopped. "I'm fine," she repeated, her voice sounding thick and choked.

Clearly, she wasn't fine.

He pushed open the door, not caring that she gasped and tried to push it closed again from where she was hunched over, sitting on the edge of the tub.

She was wrapped in one of his towels, but she was dry as a bone, her hair hanging down like a curtain, hiding her face. Obviously, she hadn't been in the shower yet at all.

"What's wrong?"

She just shook her head, not looking at him.

Alarm was growing inside him. "Emily." He crouched down in front of her, sliding her hair away from her face. "What is it?"

She finally looked up at him.

Her eyes were red. Her cheeks splotchy with tears. Her lips worked for a moment before any words emerged. "I got my period," she finally choked out.

Relief doused alarm. He smiled a little. "I hear that happens with women," he said gently. "It's not the end of the world."

She just stared at him, shaking her head,

tears leaking out her eyes. "You don't understand."

He really didn't. He was a guy. He had a grasp of the technical matters, but whatever it was that made women sometimes seem a little…edgy…around that time, was a mystery. "Is there something I can get for you? Anything you need?"

If anything, she began crying harder, her shoulders shaking as she buried her face in her hands. "I thought I was pregnant."

He blinked, then shook his head as if his hearing had gone faulty. "What?"

She slowly lifted her head. Wiped the towel over her face, but tears continued sliding down her cheeks. "I thought I was pregnant," she said more slowly, but no less thickly.

He hadn't misheard.

He stared at her, seeing the sheer misery on her face, while his brain scrambled to make sense of the situation. "We've always used protection and it's only been a week since that first time." The words came out sounding flat.

Accusing.

The same way the heavy stone sinking through his gut felt.

"So I'm pretty sure you didn't think you were pregnant from me," he added when she offered nothing in return except a hiccupping, muffled sob. Which meant she'd thought it was someone else who'd done that deed. "What were you planning to do? Use some advertising spin and try to convince me the baby was mine?"

Horror washed over Emily, adding to the grief she couldn't seem to stem, hearing Max's voice go from disbelief to this awful icy coldness. "No, that's not it at all. Max—"

He turned and walked out of the bathroom.

She instinctively went after him, tightening the towel around her when it started to slip.

He was in the bedroom, standing in the middle of the room, seeming to be staring at the bed. "I'd actually started to let myself think you'd be sharing this bed for a while," he muttered.

Her heart ached. She'd hoped that, too. Even when she'd feared what his reaction would be once she'd told him, she'd held on to that hope. "I wouldn't have lied to you like that," she said. "If I h-had been—" She couldn't even get out the word.

Pregnant.

Because she wasn't.

He crossed his arms over his chest, obviously unconvinced. "Why not? Courtney sure in hell did."

Courtney. The ex-girlfriend who'd lied to him about Anthony. She shook her head sharply. "No. No, this isn't like that, Max."

But he wasn't listening. "Who was he? Thought you'd said it'd been a long time since you'd had sex," he reminded. "Was that just something you figured I wanted to hear? It wasn't necessary." His voice hardened even more. "I would have still scr—"

"There wasn't anyone," she cried out. "I was artificially inseminated." She wanted to step closer to him, but everything about him—from his crossed arms to his expression that looked cast in granite—prevented her.

She took a deep breath, trying to gather some composure and failing miserably. "The same day we went to Etienne's—" her voice hitched again "—I'd had an appointment with the doctor that morning."

His brows pulled together, his eyes narrowing. "Artificially inseminated," he repeated. "With whose semen?"

She shook her head wildly. "It doesn't matter. An anonymous donor. From a cryobank in California."

"Should've just lied about being on the pill

when I asked you," he said flatly. "I'd have believed you and if the thing had took, I'd have never known the difference."

"I was going to tell you." But she knew how little her words meant.

Way too little.

Way too late.

Her hands were bunched over her chest, holding the towel up, holding her heart in. "Max, you *know* me. You have to know I wouldn't have lied and told you a baby was yours if it wasn't."

"And how would I know that, Emily?" He swore succinctly. "You sure in hell kept a pretty big damn secret, didn't you?"

Burning tears escaped her eyes all over again.

This time not because there was no baby growing inside her after all. Not because yet another one of her steps to become a mother had proven futile.

But because she knew she had no defense. He was right.

And now he was staring at her as if he hated her.

"The procedure was already planned before we got involved," she said thickly, still wanting him to understand, even though he was standing there, shaking his head, looking as if he didn't want to hear another word. "Nearly all I've done since I survived that tornado was try to bring a child into my life. It's all I've wanted." She sucked in a breath, still feeling as though something had been ripped from her arms. "It had nothing to do with you."

"It did the second you slept with me," he returned, his voice flat. "You should have told me."

"And you would have walked away." She waved her hand. "Just like you're going to walk away now," she finished hoarsely. "Aren't you." It wasn't a question but she still couldn't help praying that he'd deny it.

He didn't. "I don't believe any of this," he finally muttered.

She sank down onto the foot of the bed, too devastated to stand.

Not only had she lost the baby that had turned out to be only a wish in her mind, anyway, she'd lost Max.

All through her own selfish, cowardly, actions.

"I had it all planned out," she said dully. "I investigated adoption agencies, but the waiting lists are endless so I hired an attorney who handles private adoptions. Only none of the potential birth mothers who initially responded to us were interested in placing their baby with a single woman. So then I turned to artificial insemination. My sisters had conceived pretty easily, so why shouldn't I?"

She stared at her hands, but all she saw was Max's eyes. Shocked. Cold. "Except after having that procedure done—twice—" her voice went hoarse again "—I'm no closer to becoming a mother than I was when you held my hand and told me my future was waiting." She dashed the tears off her cheeks yet again, wondered if they'd ever stop.

But then what did it matter?

Tears. No tears. Nothing could erase the past few weeks. There was no rewind button, no do-over.

She wasn't pregnant.

And whatever chance she'd had with Max was just as big an illusion.

She heard him mutter another oath. And then suddenly he moved, yanking open a drawer and slamming it shut again.

"Here." He shoved a white, folded handkerchief into her hand that looked as if it had never once been used.

She took the soft cloth and pressed it beneath her eyes. It smelled like him.

"So you wanted to keep up with your sisters." His voice was hard. "Have a baby, too, just like them."

Fresh pain spread through her chest. "No. It was never about keeping up with them." She looked up at him. "Haven't you ever longed for something so badly that you would do just about anything to make it happen?"

He just looked at her.

Of course he had.

"I never expected *you*," she whispered. "To fall in love with you." There. She'd said it, knowing the truth of her words just as well as she knew they didn't matter. Her heart was well and truly out there, swinging in the breeze, and there was no hope that his would join hers there. "I know it's crazy and too soon. And I know I should have told you what I'd done. What my plans were. I just… I just didn't know how."

He exhaled roughly. Shoved his hands through his hair. "You want a baby that badly," he finally said. A little less flat. A little more gruff.

"Yes. I do." It was too late to matter now, but she wasn't going to hold back how deep that desire went. "More than anything."

He shook his head. "I don't."

She'd known, hadn't she?

He'd said children weren't in the cards for him and instead of taking heed, she'd just plowed on, believing that if he could resolve his feelings about Anthony, it would be all right.

Everything inside her was shaking. Splitting apart into agonizing shards.

She crumpled his handkerchief tightly inside her fist. "You don't want children because of Anthony."

"Because of everything in my life," he ground out. "This is my life here." He pointed at the floor. "I've finally got it together. No drugs. No booze. And the reason I'm able to keep it that way is because I finally stopped thinking I could have the things I can't. Like a son. Like a family."

"So what was I? Just a...good time? Entertainment for a few days?"

His jaw looked so tight it was nearly white. "Do you think I didn't know you wouldn't leave, too? Sooner or later everyone I care about does!"

She shook her head. "That's not true, Max."

"My father. My mother. Anthony." His gaze bored into hers. "You."

"I wouldn't leave if you asked me to stay," she managed carefully.

"Even without getting that baby you want so badly?"

Her chest squeezed. She could hardly breathe.

"See?" His voice cut through her silence. "Maybe you'd stick for a little while. At least try. But you wouldn't be able to keep from wanting more." His lips twisted. "Sooner or later, you'll head back to that corner office of yours in Atlanta and order up another donation from that place in California."

"No. You're wrong." She moistened her lips. "I won't go back to Atlanta. I resigned when I was there. I'm just an unemployed woman now."

Something came and went in his eyes. "Just another small detail you didn't think I'd be interested in knowing? Or didn't you know how to bring that up, either?"

She winced, feeling as if his words were nails sealing a coffin. "I told you I wasn't good with relationships." She pushed off the bed, looked around blindly for the red dress she'd worn the day before. The dress he'd peeled off of her as if he'd been revealing something precious to him. "It's not a defense," she added.

"It's just the truth. I've never met anyone like you, Max. And it's all happened so fast that I still feel dizzy from it." Fresh tears glazed her vision. "And I know all of this is my fault. You've done nothing to deserve any of this."

She finally spotted the fabric sticking out from beneath the jeans he'd worn the day before and snatched it up, jerking it over her head before dropping the towel she'd held clutched around her. She yanked the full skirt down around her knees and picked up the towel, nearly tripping herself in the process. She folded it in half and left it on the bed. "I should have told you. And if I couldn't do that, I should never have gotten involved with you." She didn't look at him. Couldn't bear to. "I just couldn't seem to do either. I am so, so very sorry."

"I'm sorry, too." His voice was low.

The words seemed to echo around the bedroom.

Final.

"I... I don't have a car here," she finally said.

For a long moment, he said nothing. And then he headed out of the bedroom. "I'll get my keys."

She sank her teeth into her lip, choking back the pain.

If the only thing left that she could give him was to remove herself from his life with some measure of tattered dignity, then that's what she would do.

She wiped her eyes one more time with his handkerchief, folded it carefully along the original creases back into a square and left it on his dresser. Then she found her shoes and her purse, rigidly keeping her gaze from straying to the bed. His bed. Which she'd never share again.

She straightened her shoulders and she followed him out of the apartment. Down the stairs. To his truck.

The sun was bright, the sky clear, the sweeping display of flowers at the entrance of the apartment complex's parking lot full and vibrant.

Proof that a perfectly beautiful summer day didn't care at all about a broken heart.

"Here." Tanner handed Max a stack of small, square envelopes. "Make sure these get to the controllers over in the tower, would you? They're invitations to the launch party next week. Didn't put anyone's names on them, so just give 'em out to anyone you see there and tell them to pass it on."

Max took the stack. "Anyone else?" He glanced across at Tanner, who was sitting behind his office desk at the flight school.

"Probably," Tanner muttered, flipping through the pages-long list he was studying. "Seems like we've already invited everyone in Red Rock to this shindig, but Jordana keeps reminding me of someone else we shouldn't miss."

Max's gaze drifted to the framed photographs on the credenza behind his boss's desk. One of them was of Tanner's wife. Her hair was darker than Emily's. Her eyes brown. But there was still a resemblance if you looked.

And looking was as pointless as probing a sore tooth and a helluva lot more painful.

He jerked his gaze away. Focused instead on Tanner's list. The launch party was going to be held right there at the hangar on the Fourth of July. A traditional Texas barbecue, with games for the kids and tours of the hangar, as well as a chance to see the fancy new executive jets that were already booked for charters six months in advance. "What about Gary's son and his family?"

Tanner flipped a few pages. "Jack. Taken care of already."

Max nodded. Fanned the invitations in his hand and checked the time on his watch. "I'll run these over now." He'd be back before the last set of applicants for the receptionist position were due to come in.

The stack of four hundred resumes had risen to five hundred sixty-two. He'd read every one of them.

Not hard to do when he hadn't been able to spend so much as five minutes in his own bed anymore. Since Emily left, he'd been bunking on the couch, and not sleeping much there, either.

The bright spot was that the resumes had been culled and Max was interviewing the last three candidates that afternoon.

Tanner was nodding. "While you're over at the terminal, see if you can make some headway with the maintenance supervisor on getting all that construction equipment cleared before the party. We're going to need the parking space available."

"Will do." Max turned to go.

"And Max—"

He paused, waiting.

Tanner looked at him. His dark gaze seemed

vaguely uncomfortable, which was pretty unsual for the straightforward former Air Force man. "I didn't want to mention it, but Jordana's been asking me every day."

And what Jordana wanted, Tanner tried his level best to provide. Max had seen that for himself. "Mention what?"

"Emily's refusing to come to the party," Tanner finally said abruptly. "Naturally, Jordana wants her there, but Emily says she's not doing anything that makes you uncomfortable."

Max sucked down every speck of emotion that he could.

It had been well over a week since he'd driven Emily back to her sister's.

At the time, it had felt like he'd been driving to his own funeral.

She'd sat, rigid and quiet, not crying a single tear though her face was still splotchy. When he'd pulled up in front of Wendy and Marcos's house, she'd pushed open the door and looked back at him, her eyes like bruises. "Thank you for driving me," she'd said, before slipping off the seat and closing the door. "It was very kind of you."

Finishing school polite, that was his Emily Fortune.

Only she wasn't his. Never had been, even when he'd let himself think she was. And now he knew she never would be.

He could have gotten past her withholding the fact that she'd been trying to get pregnant. Once the shock started to abate, he was reasonable enough to understand her motivation, even if he wished to heaven that she'd been honest with him.

But it didn't change the end result.

She wanted babies more than she wanted him.

Choice made. End of discussion.

End of everything.

He moved his shoulders in a careless shrug. "Doesn't matter one way or the other to me," he told Tanner.

His boss studied him for a long moment, obviously deciding whether or not to believe him. Then he finally nodded and looked back at his list. "Okay."

Max left, feeling more like it was an escape. He swiftly crossed the tarmac toward the terminal, using his ID to get through the employee entrance. He'd hunt down the maintenance supervisor before taking one of the airport trucks out to the tower.

He made his way through the terminal,

hating that every time he saw a woman with white-gold hair, he wanted to do a double take. Emily wasn't going to come back and tell him that she was wrong. That he, and he alone, would be enough for her.

He lengthened his stride even more, focusing harder on the square invitations in his hands than the healthy activity of travelers passing through, just wanting to get to the maintenance office as quickly as he could. The big, colorful beach ball that came out of nowhere rolled right across his path, his foot connecting solidly and sending it careening ahead of him.

He muffled a curse, automatically glancing around for the ball's owner as he jogged forward, catching the thing before someone accidentally tripped over it. Palming the blow-up ball, he looked around for the culprit who'd let it loose.

"Sorry, Max. So sorry!" Kelsey Fortune was trotting toward him, her auburn hair bouncing against the backpack she had hitched over her arm. She reached him and held out her hands for the ball. "I warned Coop that bringing the ball was going to be a nuisance." Her smile was bright. Either oblivious or polite enough to overlook the way Max had stiffened. "He figured it would help entertain Anthony on the plane," she went on. "I've already dropped it twice, if you can believe it."

Max handed over the ball, his gaze cutting past her. But he saw no sign of Coop or the man's son. "Taking a trip?"

She nodded and looked up at him. Even wearing cowboy boots with her dark blue jeans, she wasn't a tall woman. "Just over to California for a few days." Her lips tilted even more. "Disneyland. And frankly, I can't wait to see Cooper fit himself into the Dumbo ride with Anthony."

Despite everything, Max found the thought vaguely amusing, himself. Cooper wasn't as tall as Max was, but the rancher had the shoulders of a linebacker. "Sounds like a good time."

"Yeah."

A squeal brought their heads around. "Mama!"

And suddenly, a short, dark-haired bullet appeared, streaking between the legs of anyone who stood between him and his intended target.

Max stared, watching the little boy's chubby calves beneath the comically large cargo shorts he wore pump in concert with his fisted hands and arms. He was only peripherally aware of Cooper Fortune following hard on the tot's heels as the kid steamrolled right up to Kelsey's legs, plowing into her with all the might he had.

Max automatically shot up an arm to keep her from being knocked over by the pint-size bulldozer.

But, evidently, Kelsey was used to such exuberance, and held her ground, just dumping her backpack on the ground and sweeping up the little boy high in her arms, instead.

And then Max found himself staring at a pair of dark brown eyes that stared straight back.

A year could bring a lot of changes to a little boy.

Anthony had been just an infant when Max handed him over to the police. And even though Max could still see in Anthony's face the baby he'd been—the one Max had fumbled through bottle feedings and diaper changes with, not knowing what the hell he was doing at first—now that baby had shiny little white teeth poking out of his grinning gums, and was running.

"Man!" The shout burst out of Anthony, as if he only had one sound level, loud.

It startled Max nearly as much as the chubby hand that Anthony waved out to pat against Max's face.

"Yes, that's a man," Kelsey was laughing, though the look she shot Max was uncertain.

Cooper stopped next to them. He was carrying a backpack, too, as well as a cumbersome-looking child safety seat. "He's just stopped calling every guy he sees—" he suddenly broke off when his wife hissed a soft "Coop" from the corner of her mouth.

"Daddy," Max guessed, probing for that old ache, as well, and not finding it quite as easily as he expected. Probably because it was buried under the other pain.

The Emily pain.

Kelsey was nodding. "And instead is calling them *man*," she finished. Her smile was sympathetic as she pressed her cheek against Anthony's shoulder.

Anthony, however, had quickly turned his attention from one "man" to his father. "Daddeeeeeeeeeee," he squealed, reaching out for Cooper.

Max couldn't help but smile a little. "Looks like he's got it down," he observed and Kelsey laughed, nodding.

Cooper took his son, hefting him up to his

shoulder where Anthony latched on to his daddy's hair like he'd done it hundreds of times before. The resemblance between the two was plain for anyone to see.

"He, uh, he looks good," Max told them. "I like the shirt." He nodded toward Anthony who wore a Rangers T-shirt tucked into his big-boy cargos.

"Cooper took him to Opening Day," Kelsey said. "I think he's a little disappointed that Anthony hasn't managed 'eh-batter-eh' yet."

Max reached up and shook Anthony's hand. "You gonna be a ball player, Tony, as well as a rancher like your dad?"

Anthony grinned and swatted Max's hand. An eighteen-month-old high five, he guessed. "I can't believe how much he's grown."

"You wouldn't believe how much he eats, either," Coop said. "Kid's gonna send me to the poorhouse feeding him at Disneyland."

"Right." Max opened his palm, letting Anthony swat it again. They were there to catch a flight, not just roam the walls of the Red Rock terminal. Max gently bumped his palm against Anthony's one last time and started to move away. His throat was tightening. "You guys have a great time."

"We will." Cooper looked like he wanted to

say something. For that matter so did Kelsey. But after a moment, she just reached down and picked up her backpack and tucked the ball under her arm, and the couple turned to go.

Anthony craned around, grinning at Max as they went. He lifted his hand, his fingers opening and closing.

Max started to wave back. Realized he was still holding the party invitations.

"Coop." The word shot out of his mouth before he could take time to regret it.

The other man stopped. Turned around. "Yeah?"

"Here." He headed forward, held out one of the invitations. "We're having a barbecue on the Fourth of July," he said. "Over at the flight school. Celebrating the holiday as well as our launch of Redmond Charter. If you're back, maybe you and your…family…will think about coming." His gaze strayed to Anthony. The kid was blowing raspberries now, his cheeks puffing out like a chipmunk. "There'll be plenty of barbecue," he added, chuckling a little. "Bring a container and stock up for the little guy."

Cooper reached out slowly and took the envelope. "Thanks, Max." He smiled slowly. "We'll be there."

Not entirely sure what he'd done, except that he was oddly glad he'd done it, Max nodded toward the travelers starting to congest around the security gate. "You'd better get moving," he advised. "New security crew. They're thorough as heck but *slow*. You wouldn't want to miss the Dumbo ride."

"Dum-moh!" Anthony latched on the word, yelling it at the top of his lungs. He slapped his hands down on Cooper's head. "Dum-moh!"

"Thanks," Cooper said dryly. "You had to say the D-word, didn't you?" He lifted his hand, sketching a wave, and turned with his wife.

Max watched them go, listening to Anthony's young voice chanting louder than all of the noise in the terminal combined.

And finally, knowing that he had to get to the maintenance office and the tower before his interviewees arrived, he turned away.

But for the first time in over a week, he felt a smile on his face. And this one wasn't forced.

Chapter 13

"Ms. Fortune. This is Joanna at the Armstrong Fertility Institute. We've had a cancellation in our schedule next week and would be able to fit you in for your initial consultation if you're available. Please call me right away at area code six-one—"

Emily pressed a button on her phone, deleting the voice mail message that she'd already listened to twice.

"Come on." Wendy nudged her shoulder from behind. "Jordana's gonna skin us alive if we're any later than we already are, and Marcos is waiting with the baby in the car."

Emily stood up from the kitchen chair where

she'd been sitting and unlooped the bulging diaper bag from her sister's arm so she wouldn't have to juggle that as well as the stacks of pink bakery boxes containing the pastries she'd prepared for the picnic. The reason they were late was because Wendy kept changing her mind about what she might or might not need to take for MaryAnne. "Are you sure there's nothing else we need to grab? Maybe the kitchen sink, too?"

Wendy made a face and carefully moved through the front door so as not to disturb her baked cargo. "Make sure it's locked." She started down the few shallow steps toward the sidewalk.

Emily set the lock and followed.

She still felt certain that she shouldn't be going to Tanner's big party. But Jordana kept insisting that she and Tanner needed more help with all of the activities they'd planned and Emily couldn't very well refuse, even if the thought of running into Max was nearly more than she could stand.

If Jordana was to be believed, Max had specifically said he didn't mind that Emily would be there.

She didn't dare let herself read too much into that. If Max had said *no,* she would have honored it, and taken her lumps with Jordana. But he hadn't.

She realized that Wendy was waiting for her at the car, obviously needing assistance, and she hurried forward. "Sorry." She helped her sister settle the boxes securely in the trunk, then climbed in the backseat where MaryAnne was already positioned, sound asleep, in her car seat.

"Okay," Wendy said, a little breathlessly as she got in, too, and quietly closed her car door. "Good to go." All of them had been tiptoeing around for hours, hoping the baby would get a really good nap in before the barbecue, when the noise and commotion was likely to keep her awake for hours.

Emily stared out the window, feeling her nerves tighten a little more with every block they passed, until she felt vaguely nauseated. She rolled the window down a little until she felt the blow of air on her forehead.

"Have you heard anything about the offer you made on the house, Emily?"

Emily looked over at Marcos and caught his gaze in the rearview mirror. "Not yet," she told him. "My Realtor gave them until tomorrow night to accept or counter." She'd settled on the little house on the hill. Even though the nursery wouldn't likely be used now, it was still the most appealing place she'd looked at. Max might have ended things, but Emily still needed a place to live. And the steps needed to arrange buying one had given her something to fill her days with.

The nights, though, just stayed endless and empty.

"With any luck, you'll have your guest bedroom back within few weeks," she added.

"You know we haven't minded you staying with us," Marcos said.

Emily managed to smile slightly in response, before looking out the window once more. They were turning into the main entrance of the airport.

Her smile faded. Nerves returned.

Even before Marcos reached the parking lot in front of the flight school, they could see the enormous red, white and blue balloons that stretched high into the sky, bobbing and waving in the breeze. There was even one of those enormous inflatable houses that kids bounced in and Emily knew from Jordana there were other games and entertainment planned for the children. Thanks to Wendy's dithering, they were more than a half hour late, and there was already a crowd of people milling around the grassy area as well as the open bays of the hangar. If the early turnout was any indication, the afternoon would be an unqualified success.

Marcos left them off near the lawn before going in search of an open parking spot since the lot was clearly full. Emily managed to carry all of MaryAnne's gear *and* push the stroller they'd fastened her carrier into while Wendy carried her pastry boxes ahead of her, aiming for the tented area where the food was located.

Alongside the tent, the largest barbecue setup Emily had ever seen was being manned by a couple of men wearing white aprons wrapped around their waists, and every time they opened one of the doors to the barrel-looking contraption, the mouthwatering scent of barbecue escaped.

It even made Emily feel a little hungry, and she hadn't felt like eating since Max had left her at the curb in front of Wendy's house.

"Emily!"

She heard her name through the cacophony of music and childish shrieks and craned her head around, searching for the source. She finally found it in her cousin, Victoria, who was standing on a folding lawn chair, waving madly at her.

Emily hitched the Fold-N-Play under her arm a little higher and maneuvered the stroller across the thick grass, working her way around tables and chairs and blankets spread on the ground where people were already picnicking.

She could feel beads of sweat working down her back when she finally made it to Victoria and knew they were just as likely caused by the effort not to think about the picnic blanket she'd shared with Max as they were from the afternoon's heat.

Victoria was beaming at her and her cousin hopped off her chair, bouncing over to give Emily a hug before peeking beneath the canopy shading MaryAnne in the stroller. "She just gets prettier every time I see her," Victoria pronounced as she straightened and waved toward the very tall man who'd risen from his own lawn chair when Emily approached. "Garrett, honey." Victoria gestured toward her fiancé. "Help Emily unload, would you?"

The good-looking rancher smiled faintly, and nodded at Emily in greeting as he quickly slipped the Fold-N-Play from her unsteady grip.

"Thanks." She pulled the diaper bag off the back of the stroller and set it on the ground because she was afraid it was too heavy and would tip the whole multi-wheeled contraption right over, MaryAnne included. "I didn't even think to bring a lawn chair," she admitted, looking over the crowd.

Victoria just waved a hand. "Don't worry," she said. "Jordana says they've nearly rented out the town's supply of 'em." Her brown curls bouncing, she looked up at her tall fiancé. "Garrett, honey—"

"I got it," he said, looking amused, and set off, working his way through the congestion far more easily than Emily had.

"Just because you can bat those big brown eyes of yours at that man and he seems ready to jump to your bidding doesn't mean you had to send him off for a chair for me," Emily told her cousin wryly. "I could've gone and got one myself."

Victoria made a face. "Max was over there, last I saw."

Hearing his name made everything inside Emily take a slow, swooping dip. She quickly shoved her hands into the hidden side pockets of her green sundress before Victoria could see them shaking. Her fingertips worried the small links of the daisy bracelet she'd tucked there. Unable to put it away, but unable to wear it. "It wouldn't have mattered," she lied to her diminutive cousin.

Victoria just gave her a look as if she knew better. Since she and Wendy were close, and Emily knew Victoria was also thick as thieves with Jordana, perhaps she did know.

"Tanner's got to be pleased with the turnout today," she said, anxious to move away from the topic of Max. "I see so many Fortunes around you'd think it was a family reunion."

"Right?" Victoria's head bobbed. "Garrett saw the crowd and wanted to turn around and head back to Pete's Retreat." She smiled, oozing sweet, Southern charm. "I, of course, convinced him not to."

Emily couldn't help but laugh. Her cousin's infectiousness always had that ability. "I really should go find Jordana and check in with her." Emily glanced under the canopy to see that MaryAnne, miraculously, was still sound asleep. "She's been haranguing me for days that she had too many tasks to fill with too few able bodies."

"She's got me scooping ice cream, of all things," Victoria said. "Once they bring it on out. Last I saw, she was over by Tanner's pretty new jets." She waved her hands in a shooing motion. "Go on and find her. I can watch MaryAnne. I'm hoping if Garrett keeps seeing me minding her, it'll give him ideas." Her eyes sparkled.

Her cousin had no way of knowing how her words hurt. Emily managed a quick thanks before heading in the direction of the hangar bays, bracing herself even more as she went.

With every step she took closer to the planes, her anxiety grew, feeling like Max was going to pop out of nowhere at any second. Which was ludicrous. He wouldn't be hunting around for her, that was for certain.

She left the grass and crossed the tarmac, her gaze straying over to the tie-down area where the plane he'd flown the day of their picnic had been parked. The small, white and green plane wasn't there today, though. She didn't know if she was relieved, or sad.

Tanner's jets—two of them—were parked next to each other, their placement right at the yawning opening of the hangar doors, showing them off as the obvious guests of honor. The cabin doors were open, the stairs extended for people to head up inside and explore the luxury. She rounded the line of people waiting at the nearest one, her eyes hunting for her sister.

"Emily!" Tanner waved from inside the

shade of the hangar. "Jordana's got stuff set up in the classrooms."

She nodded and angled toward the door that she knew, courtesy of Max's tour, would lead her there. She brushed her hands down the front of her sundress, took a deep breath and went inside. But even then, she didn't run into Max along the way. Just reached her sister, who was pointing hither and yon, directing a small group of people Emily didn't recognize, and looking like she was ready to tear out her hair.

Spotting her, Jordana shooed the others off to their assignments and turned on her. "Finally! Where's Wendy? She brought her desserts, didn't she?"

Emily nodded. "Don't stress out any more than you already are. Wendy's delivering the goods over to the food area and I'm here to help with whatever you need."

Jordana blew out a puff of air that stirred her hair. "Good. Okay." She waddled to a table piled high with boxes that had been pushed against one wall. "These toys, believe it or not, need to be wrapped." She picked up a roll of red, white and blue wrapping paper. There were dozens of similar rolls sticking out of a crate next to the table. "The store that do-

nated them said they'd come wrapped but…
obviously not. There's scissors and tape and as
soon as I can find someone else to help you,
I'll send 'em over."

"Why do you need to wrap them?" Emily
picked up one of the toys. It was already pack-
aged, albeit not in the red, white and blue colors of the day. But Jordana gave her a look,
and Emily snatched up the scissors. "Don't
worry," she said quickly. "What are you using
them for?" There had to be at least a hundred
of the boxes. "How soon do you need them?"

"Game prizes for the kids. And the sooner
the better." Jordana shook her head, heading
off. "They were just supposed to already be
wrapped," she was muttering.

Emily blew out a breath, studied the over-
loaded table for a moment before dragging over
another table that wasn't being used. When it
was positioned to her liking, she retrieved a
few of the large empty boxes discarded hap-
hazardly in one corner of the classroom, and
positioned them beneath the table. Then she
unrolled the first roll of wrapping paper. Got
an idea of how large a piece she needed. The
toys looked like they were different items, but
the boxes they came in were all pretty much
the same size. And she leaned over her work

surface and began cutting. And cutting. And cutting. She'd cut and stacked enough squares of paper to empty six rolls of the wrapping paper when she judged that sufficient enough to make some significant headway. Then she grabbed the roll of tape and plopped a toy in the center of the first paper square.

"Looks like you've got an organized plan there."

She straightened, whirling around to face Max. Her heart felt like it shot to her throat, dropped to her toes and shot back up again all in the moment it took for her gaze to race over his face. Did he look thinner? His eyes tired? "What are you doing here?"

He plucked at the front of his Redmond Flight School polo. "Work here," he said, his voice deadly dry.

She flushed. "I meant in here." Tired or thinner or not, he still looked so wonderful to her that her chest ached. "Shouldn't you be out there—" she gestured vaguely "—enjoying the results of your efforts?"

He didn't answer that. Just jerked his chin toward the work table she'd organized. "Jordana was looking for help."

Emily quickly spun around again, facing the paper and the toys. He hadn't come to find *her.* Of course not. Wanting to throttle her sister, she blindly tore off a length of tape only to have it fold over and stick to itself, useless. She made a noise and shook it off her thumb to start again. "I'm sure she can find someone with less important tasks than you have to help with this."

"I offered."

Her hand trembled. She pressed it on top of the covered gift and sealed the paper with the tape. "I'm sorry." She turned the gift. Folded paper. Sealed again and dropped it in the box before grabbing the next toy. "She should have warned you I was here."

"I knew."

"I see." But she didn't. Not at all.

She focused hard on her task. Plop toy. Fold paper. Slap some tape on. If Emily worked fast enough, Jordana would have the toys—maybe not perfectly wrapped, but still wrapped—by the time she needed them. Without looking at Max, she divided her stack of pre-cut sheets and set some to the side for him. "All of the tape is over there." She'd stacked the rolls so that she could grab them easily when she ran out. She muttered an oath when she ruined another piece of tape.

"Here." Max lifted the tape dispenser out of her hand. "You wrap. I'll give you the tape."

She casually hid her hand in the folds of her skirt and tried to rub away the tingling inside her fingers. "Fine. Give me a piece of tape, then. It doesn't need to be very long. Maybe an inch, inch and a half. Otherwise I'm afraid we'll run out before—"

"You *are* bossy."

She snapped her lips together and watched him tear off a piece of tape, quite deliberately, at least four inches long. He gave it to her and she slapped it onto the paper, dropping the finished product into the box. Without a word, she reached for the next toy but her nerves had already reached such a screaming pitch she couldn't stand it. She whirled on him. "If you didn't want me to be here, you should have just told Tanner that! I would have stayed home."

"Who said I didn't want you to be here?" His smooth tone gave absolutely nothing away.

"Obviously, you don't."

"I'm helping you, aren't I?"

She stared. He was using an overly reasonable tone that wormed right beneath her skin. "I don't need your help. As you pointed out, I have an organized plan here."

"Plans *can* be shared."

She inhaled, feeling like she'd been hit below the belt. "I'm sorry. I've told you I'm sorry. I shouldn't have lied to you. Shouldn't have kept what I was doing a secret."

"No," he agreed. He reached past her for one of the boxes, his arm brushing against hers, and placed it in the center of the paper. "But I am able to see how that might have been…awkward at first." He tore off three short pieces of tape and made fast work out of fastening all the perfectly folded sides before dropping the wrapped toy in the box.

Much more efficiently, and certainly much faster, than she'd been doing.

"I worked in a department store over Christmas once," he said and handed her back the tape. "One of my many jobs in my misspent youth."

Her mind felt pinched with memories. She turned back to the toys. Mimicked Max's method. The end result was a little neater. She grabbed another toy. "It would be easier to do this alone," she said huskily. "And I know you *must* have more important things to do."

"Maybe." He was silent for a moment. "What's the next step in your plan? Your pregnancy plan. You going to have another artificial—" He waved his hand, not finishing.

She gnawed at the inside of cheek and shook her head. "No."

"Why not?"

Her shoulders bowed. "Do you really want the details?" She didn't wait for an answer, but shook her head. "I haven't decided what I'm going to do." She, who hadn't dithered over decision making since she was a schoolgirl, and maybe not even then, couldn't seem to make one single plan in that regard.

"Pursue adoption some more?"

She forced herself to grab another toy, not answering.

"Tanner says you made an offer on a house."

"Tanner talks a lot," she muttered, feeling too wounded inside to dwell on how surprising that actually was. Tanner *wasn't* a big talker. But then what did she know about how close Tanner and Max were becoming? They worked together every day.

"Did you mean it when you said you loved me?"

She felt an ominous burning behind her eyes.

She hadn't let herself cry since that day in Max's bedroom.

If he wanted a pound of flesh, she would give it. "Yes." She pressed her molars together, finished another toy and dropped it in the box. But when she reached for the next toy, her hand wouldn't go. She stared down at the paper. Realized her hands were clenched into fists. "If I could go back and change anything, Max, I would."

"What would you change? Going to Red? Etienne's? My place? Flying? What?"

She closed her eyes. She wouldn't give up the memory of any one of those moments with him. Not when they were all she had left. "I wouldn't have had the A.I," she said huskily.

"Why? You want a baby. More than anything, you said."

She couldn't take it. The pain inside her was excruciating. "If I hadn't done it, maybe I would still have you." She stared at the toys that Jordana was so insistent about having wrapped and decided that her sister would have to be disappointed. She set down the tape and walked away, blindly heading in the general direction of the door that led back to the hangar, because she couldn't see through the tears glazing her eyes. Her hands felt the crash bar and she pushed, door swinging wide, and escaped into the hangar, breaking into a run and not caring that the people standing in line to view Tanner's new jets were turning to look.

"Emily. Wait!"

She could hardly hear anything over the rushing sound inside her head, but she still heard his voice.

She almost kept running.

But she lived in Red Rock now. Sooner or later she was bound to run into him again. It was the same poignant promise—just as much a curse—that had dominated her thoughts, coming to the launch party.

But she stopped. Looked back at him, watching him stride through the hangar toward her, and it took everything she possessed to lift her chin and square her shoulders, slide her hands inside her dress pockets and wait. Not to show herself as utterly destroyed as she felt inside.

But his blue gaze searched her face, as if he saw right through her. He stopped several feet away. "I thought the hardest thing I'd ever do in my life was admitting that Anthony wasn't mine."

She trembled, the edge of a tiny metal daisy pressed against her palm.

He took a step closer. She saw a muscle flex in his jaw. "Thought that if I never expected anything from anyone else...never counted on anyone else… I'd be okay. And I'd never have to face something like that again."

"Max—"

He lifted his hand. "Let me."

She pressed her lips together, her throat going tight. She wasn't even sure what she'd wanted to say, how to articulate the emotion roiling inside her chest.

"You threw me for a loop, Emily Fortune. From that very first afternoon you looked at me in Tanner's office. And even though I'd told myself you never would, you recognized me from the day of the tornado. From then, right up until the morning you stood in my apartment, crying in front of me because you were devastated that you weren't pregnant, you've kept me off balance. One minute you're a corner-office advertising whiz and the next you're a girl who cartwheels in the grass—"

"Badly," she inserted on the sad half laugh that bubbled out of her.

"—who blushes when I tell her she's beautiful, but can seduce me with nothing more than a look. Whether it's been my own doing or not, nothing much has come easy in my life. But it was easy falling in love with you."

She went still. Her gaze latched on to his.

He was shaking his head, even as he took

another slow step toward her. "You're a Fortune. You're rich. Educated. Way more than I deserve."

"You're the one who deserves everything," she whispered. "I'm the one who—"

"Had a plan."

She pressed her lips together, gathering what shreds of composure she could. "I'm thirty years old, Max. Who gets to be thirty years old before they fall in love for the first time in her life? After the tornado, I knew I couldn't wait around any longer. If I was going to have someone of my own—a child of my own—I had to take action." She gulped down a harsh breath. "If I'd only come to Tanner's office and met you earlier. Realized that the perfect match for me that I'd never believed existed… did—" She broke off. Shook her head.

He'd stopped in front of her. Close enough to touch. But not touching. "You shouldn't have to give up your dream of becoming a mother for anyone, Emily. Not even me."

She sucked down the pain. "Don't," she whispered. "I know everything ended that day at your apartment. We don't need to do it again."

"I sure as hell hope not," he agreed roughly

and grabbed her wrists, pulling her hands out of her pockets.

The daisy bracelet he'd given her dangled from her clenched fingers.

Max saw and exhaled a long, shuddering breath. He slowly worked it out of her clutch, even though she held on tightly, as if she were afraid to let go. "This I what I can give you," he said, holding the bracelet in front of her. "If there are diamonds, they're a long way off. And if admitting Anthony wasn't mine was hard, facing a future without you in it is a million times worse." He lifted her hand and dropped the bracelet in her palm. The little white daisy glinted before it disappeared beneath her fingers that he folded over it. Then he wrapped his hand around hers and looked into her eyes—her lovely peridot eyes that were shimmering with tears as she stared up at him.

"I don't know anymore how to feel about having kids, but I do know that I love you, Emily. And maybe, if we just give this a chance—this thing between us—I'll be able to figure it out along the way, because I can't stand knowing you don't have everything you want. So if it comes to a choice between having you, and all of your plans, whatever they are, or not having you at all—" his voice went hoarse "—the past few weeks of hell has shown me there's no choice at all."

Her forehead crumpled. "But I lied to you. How can you ever trust—"

He slid his hand through her silky hair, tilting back her head and she went abruptly silent, lips parted. "You didn't tell me everything," he said huskily. "And it hurt like hell. But things were moving fast. Full disclosure was probably more than either one of us could expect."

"Now you're just excusing it."

"I didn't tell you I fell in love with you that day we went flying." He watched her pupils dilate at the admission. "Didn't tell you everything about Anthony." He brushed his thumb over her cheek. Saw the way her eyes flickered. "We both could have said more than we did and we didn't. The question is whether that ends now and we move forward or not."

"Forward?" The word was little more than a breath. "You still want to see me?"

"See you." He smiled faintly. "Laugh with you." His thumb grazed down her satin-smooth cheek. Brushed over her lips. "Make love with you. Live with you."

Her eyes widened. "Live with me?"

"That's usually what husbands and wives do," he murmured with painful casualness.

Her lips parted. He felt her trembling and gathered her against him, sliding his arms around her and feeling almost whole again for the first time in weeks when her hands crept up between them, her fingertips dazedly touching his cheek.

"I'm not that great of a catch," she warned. "In the interest of full disclosure and everything. I still don't have a job. And Wendy kicked me out of the kitchen at Red when she was trying to teach me how to bake chocolate croissants. I'm probably worse than Mrs. Sheckley when it comes to baking."

"You're also a bed hog." He closed her fingers in his hand and kissed her fingertips. "Which is fine with me as long as I'm the one in the bed you're hogging. Plus, I've gotten sorta fond of Mrs. Sheckley's baking. Now stop trying to debate this and just tell me you'll marry me."

"Now who's sounding bossy?"

"Emily—"

Emily stared into Max's face, hardly daring to breathe, her heart was so full. He'd once told her that her future was waiting for her to live it. She didn't know anymore what that future would hold. But she finally knew that it didn't matter.

Because the future was right now, and he was holding her in his arms so closely that she could feel the unsteady beat of his heart against hers.

"Yes," she whispered tremulously, going on her toes to press her lips against his. "Yes, Max, I'll marry you."

Epilogue

"*Whoa*. Hold up there, buddy." Max reached out and caught Anthony by the scruff of his neck before he could plow over the empty flower stand stored in the cramped office where they were holed up, earning a mutinous look from the two-year-old. He chucked the little boy lightly under his chin and tickled the front of his belly, turning mutiny to chortles in the blink of an eye.

Max grinned and straightened the bow tie the kid was wearing, but it still remained hopelessly skewed, and he gave it up, not particularly caring. That's what they got for trying to put a toddler in a tuxedo and tie, even minia-ture-size ones.

"Okay." Jeremy strode into the room. "Got the license." He patted his lapel pocket. "Got the rings." He grinned at little Anthony. "Got the best men." His grin traveled to take in Max. "Got the groom."

"As long as there's a bride," he muttered, running his finger beneath the collar of his shirt, then having to go check the mirror again to make sure that his own tie wasn't lopsided.

"There's a bride all right," Jeremy assured. He shot his cuffs, looking as comfortable in his formal wear as Max wasn't. "Saw her with my own eyes." He grinned. "Good thing I'm married to your sister."

"Good thing Emily's your cousin," Max re-minded.

"Second. Third. Something like that." Jer-emy chuckled.

"Good God, it's a zoo out there." Scott, Em-ily's second oldest brother, rushed into the room. He, too, was wearing a tux.

"Get used to it," Max advised. "Yours and Christina's wedding won't be any different.

Scott made a face. "After today, I'm think-ing eloping sounds good."

"But you won't." Tanner had overheard as

he and Emily's other two brothers, Blake and Michael, came into the room.

"Nope," Blake agreed. He was Max's age and his dark eyes were amused. "You won't disappoint the woman you love any more than I'd ever want to disappoint Katie."

"You guys gonna wax poetic about love or are we gonna get this wedding going, so we can move on to the party?" Michael, the eldest of Emily and her siblings, made no secret that he had no interest in such things. In the past week since all of the Fortunes had come to Red Rock to celebrate Christmas and prepare for his and Emily's New Year's Eve wedding, Max had seen for himself that Michael—demanding and blunt—was pretty much a carbon copy of John Michael. "I'm ready for the company of any pretty ladies who go for a guy in a monkey suit."

"I'm ready," Max admitted. Not because he wanted to get to the reception, which Emily had planned with military precision along with the elaborate wedding, but because he wanted to get on with the honeymoon. And that was something he'd planned. Keeping the details a surprise from her hadn't been easy, though. Not only was Emily bossy; she was relentless when there was something she wanted to know. And her methods of persuasion had been becoming increasingly...persuasive lately.

"All right then." Jeremy picked up Anthony, who happily started plucking at the white petals on his boutonniere. He was used to his "uncle" Jeremy since Kirsten and he had never stopped maintaining contact with him. Max's sister wasn't part of the wedding party, but as his only family, she'd be sitting in the front pew on his side of the church, directly across from Emily's parents, and would be ready to help distract Anthony, along with Coop and Kelsey who were supposed to be in the row behind his sister.

In fact, once the Reverend Peterson came into the office, lined them up and marched them out to the front of the church where violin music played, Max could only think that the church pews were filled only with Fortunes of one sort or another. Cousins. Uncles. Nieces. They weren't only in the pews, they were in the wedding party.

Even now, Emily's sisters appeared and began gliding up the aisle, looking striking in deep blue dresses.

He caught Mrs. Sheckley's eye where she was sitting next to his sister in the front pew.

She beamed at him, smiling just as brightly as Emily's mother.

And then the music changed, sliding seamlessly from a host of violins to a church organ.

Everyone in the pews shuffled, rose and turned to watch. Max thought his heart might just bust out of his tux as he waited for her to appear.

And then, there she was, taking her father's arm as she turned toward Max. Her hair was pulled back in a sleek ponytail and she looked slender, ethereal. And so incredibly beautiful that the entire church seemed to inhale as one at the sight of her.

Her gaze was locked on his face, a smile on her own as she walked down the aisle with her father. Turning her head a little so John Michael could kiss her cheek just as they'd rehearsed the night before when she reached Max's side.

Unlike the rehearsal the night before, though, Max was almost shocked to see the dampness in the older man's eyes as he placed Emily's hand in Max's. He gave Max a sharp nod, then turned and joined his wife in the pew. Max figured it wouldn't be long before John Michael adjusted to the fact that his daughter had struck out on her own, doing freelance advertising—though the afternoon before he'd been bugging Emily to at least *consider* the idea of working for FortuneSouth again. Particularly since he'd decided that a satellite office in Red Rock was just what the company needed.

Max was vaguely aware of the minister talking but he was too busy drowning in the smile that Emily was giving him over her bouquet of daisies. And then she was handing off that bouquet to Jordana and taking Max's hands in hers, turning to face him. His thumb roved over her wrist, feeling the sterling daisy bracelet there, as it had been nearly every day since the Fourth of July.

The minister was going on about the duties of marriage and Emily's eyes sparkled up at Max. "Have I told you today that I love you?" she whispered.

"Once or twice." Particularly that very morning in their bedroom on the hillside house where they lived.

Reverend Peterson slid them a disapproving look but plowed on.

"Are you going to tell me where we're going for our honeymoon, yet?" She still kept her voice low. "For all I know, I've packed all the wrong clothes."

Reverend Peterson cleared his throat, giving them another look. He held up the Bible in his hands that he was reading from, and continued.

"A picnic," Max whispered. "In each state from here on up to Canada."

If anything, Emily's smile deepened. "Flying, I assume?"

"In a plane just built for two."

"Bliss," she whispered. Her dimple flashed and her eyes glowed. "Did you borrow Mrs. Sheckley's picnic basket?"

His hands tightened on hers. "And the blanket," he murmured, looking into her eyes and feeling like he could see forever there. "I promised her that we'd do our best to carry on her family tradition..."

* * * * *

Get 4 FREE REWARDS!

We'll send you 2 FREE Books plus 2 FREE Mystery Gifts.

Harlequin® Special Edition books feature heroines finding the balance between their work life and personal life on the way to finding true love.

FREE Value Over $20

Get 4 FREE REWARDS!

We'll send you 2 FREE Books plus 2 FREE Mystery Gifts.

Harlequin® Romance Larger-Print books feature uplifting escapes that will warm your heart with the ultimate feel-good tales.

FREE
Value Over
$20

Get 4 FREE REWARDS!

We'll send you 2 FREE Books plus 2 FREE Mystery Gifts.

FREE
Value Over
$20

Both the **Romance** and **Suspense** collections feature compelling novels written by many of today's best-selling authors.

Get 4 FREE REWARDS!

We'll send you 2 FREE Books plus 2 FREE Mystery Gifts.

Ava's Prize
Cari Lynn Webb

THE RANCHER'S FAKE FIANCÉE
Amy Vastine

Harlequin® Heartwarming™ Larger-Print books feature traditional values of home, family, community and—most of all—love.

FREE
Value Over
$20

READERSERVICE.COM

Manage your account online!

- Review your order history
- Manage your payments
- Update your address

> *We've designed the*
> *Reader Service website*
> *just for you.*

Enjoy all the features!

- Discover new series available to you, and read excerpts from any series.
- Respond to mailings and special monthly offers.
- Browse the Bonus Bucks catalog and online-only exculsives.
- Share your feedback.

Visit us at:

ReaderService.com